CU00405249

The Black Meadow Archive

Volume 1

Chris Lambert

Panel illustrations
Andy Paciorek

***Lair of the Coyle* illuminations**
Nigel Wilson

***Ghost Planes* illustrations**
John Chadwick

Front Cover
Phil Heeks

First published in Great Britain in 2019 by Exiled Publishing, South Street Arts Centre, 21 South Street, Reading, RG1 4QU

A CIP catalogue record for this book is available from the British Library

ISBN: 9781688953161

blackmeadowtales.blogspot.com
lambertthewriter.blogspot.co.uk
exiledpublications.blogspot.co.uk
soullesscentral.blogspot.com

Proofreading by Grey Malkin.

Thanks to:

Grey Malkin, Andy Paciorek, Nigel Wilson, Kev Oyston, Phil Heeks, Colin from Castles in Space, Chris Sharp, John Chadwick, The Folk Horror Revival and Bob Fischer.

Contents

List of Illustrations

Walking on the Black Meadow

Roger Mullins – The Black Meadow (1968)

In August 1972 Roger Mullins, a professor at the University of York, was reported missing. He was last seen about half a mile from RAF Fylingdales (the Nuclear Attack early warning system) by an associate from the university, who dropped him off to make some field recordings in the area. According to Professor Philip Hull, a colleague of Mullins, when this associate went to pick him up at the agreed time, there was no sign of him. A police search began three days later and no trace of his body was found.

Reports from the area, at the time of the disappearance, suggested that an unseasonal and particularly dense mist was covering this part of the

North York Moors. Whilst most would consider this of no significance, to Professor Hull and other colleagues from the university, this was a very important factor in Roger's disappearance. For it had long been said that "when the mist rises, the village comes." This village, which features in thousands of accounts about the area, comes and goes when the mist is high. Did Roger Mullins find this village? Is he still there?

According to Professor Philip Hull, Roger's obsession with the Black Meadow began when he was working as a folklorist in his native New Zealand. Roger collected stories passed down from generation to generation from the Maori tribes who lived near Christchurch. He was interested in folklore from around the world and was particularly drawn to the tales that seemed to flood the North York Moors, in particular those equating to the Black Meadow. When the offer of a post at the University of York (related to the study of local folklore) was offered to him, it was too good an opportunity to pass up.

When Roger Mullins first stepped into the mist of the North York Moors in 1964 he was following in the footsteps of Stanley Coulton and Lord Thomas Brightwater. Stanley Coulton was a collector of local folk stories and songs who lived in Boscombe, Dorset but spent every holiday (he worked as an architect for the Freemasons) in Sleights, Robin Hood's Bay and Whitby walking the moors and collecting stories between 1860 and 1912. It is said that the story "The Stone Steps" in "Tales from the Black Meadow" is loosely based on one of his experiences on the moor.[1] Coulton reported to the local press that he had found a stone circle that, no matter how much he had searched, he could not seem to rediscover. This was particularly disconcerting for him as he was a confident cartographer and explorer. He then told them that, after much searching, he had found that same stone circle but in an entirely different location. When he took the reporter to this relocated circle they could not find it. On four more occasions Coulton reported that the same circle appeared again in four different places. On each occasion he reported that the mist was high. Coulton is perhaps more famous for bringing one of the most popular Black Meadow poems to light - "Can you tell me maiden fair", that spoke of a parent's grief for a missing child.

> *"Can you tell me maiden fair,*
> *Can you tell me if or where*
> *I shall see my child again*
> *Walk upon the fields of men?*
> *Will she ever stumble back*
> *From the meadow all a'black?"*
> Can you tell me maiden fair – (Traditional)[2]

Lord Brightwater is remembered for his work investigating the Black Meadow in the 1930s. The government ordered an enquiry following the disappearances of over 30 individuals on the North

---

[1] C. Lambert, *Tales from the Black Meadow* (Reading: Exiled Publications, 2013), p.95

[2] C. Lambert, *Tales from the Black Meadow* (Reading: Exiled Publications, 2013), p.11

York Moors. His investigation lasted several years but was shut down when the government decided that the funding would be better used elsewhere.

It was the notes and records made by his team that formed the foundation of Mullins' work. These have very recently been re-opened, following the government's relaxing of public access to files that were previously limited by the Official Secrets Act. The Brightwater Archive is a privately funded group who are now publishing significant finds from the files. They have been working on this for six years and have made some significant discoveries including records of anomalous soil samples, data about missing individuals, correspondence between the investigators and Whitehall and other artefacts. It is they who are responsible for the recently erected plaque to Roger Mullins that can be found on the North York Moors, near to RAF Fylingdales where Roger Mullins was last seen.

Plaque erected by "The Brightwater Archive" in memory of Roger Mullins.

In the last few years there has been a resurgence of interest in the Black Meadow. In 2012 Kev Oyston began work on "Tales from the Black Meadow" a CD

Album that contained the soundtrack to a lost Radio 4 Documentary from the late 1970's called "Curse of the Black Meadow". He worked with writer and researcher Chris Lambert who discovered and collated a series of stories based on Roger Mullins' original findings. These were collected in "Tales from the Black Meadow". Their work was lauded by academics as well as the popular press, with reviews in magazines such as "Starburst" and articles in "Shindig". Chris Lambert has also presented papers at Queens University Belfast, Corpus Christi College Cambridge, the Explaining the Unexplainable conference in York and the British Museum about the Black Meadow phenomena.

This new collection brings together legends, tales and accounts about the Black Meadow using information gathered from the Brightwater Archive, the Coulton Estate, Roger Mullins' notes and witness statements and interviews.

Ancient Tales

Lair of the Coyle

LAIR OF THE COYLE

Taken from "Accountes from the Yorke Pilgrimage".

The next weary traveller was old and frail
 His eyes spark'd as dying coals in cooling ash
Within the dry canyon wrinkles of his face.
Upon his bald head sat a velvet cap.
A white beard adorn'd his cheeks and pointed chin
Shorn close to grey skin and fleckèd much with black.
When he spoke his voice crack'd as oldest flint
Rumbling full of phlegm, deep puddl'd i'th'throat.
His eyes, once white and clearest blue 'round black,
Were yellow, lin'd with blood fill'd creeks and
Brooks trickling fast 'round a dusty grey iris.
His cloak, pull'd tight, as like a swaddling wrap,
Hid weaken'd arms and feeblest quail bone chest,
Whilst purple breeches of warming worstèd wool
Protected childlike knees a'knocking from the chill.
He talk'd of much, so the other pilgrims thought,
To stave off cold, lonely hours saddlebound
And build perchance a braver reputation
Than outward looks betray'd to all who saw him.

So it was on the fourth night they rested
 Soft in lowly barn. Firelit. Ham on spit.
Sweet mushrooms mix'd with bubbling dumpling broth.
Bellies sated, the pilgrims let the trav'ller speak,
He ey'd them all and clear'd his fullen throat
And thus began:

One has oft heard tell of the holes that lie deep
I'th'earth, hid by briar, branch and bramble.
It is where heather grows in abundance
On the long stony path to Sleights that these holes
Lie deep, dark and deadly to unwary step
If you were to seek one out to look inside
The view would surprise, befuddle and confuse,
For black you should see, deep, darkest coal black.
But while there is darkness, beyond is a glow,
A haze, as of a crackling winter fire
Breaking the blackness with a golden shine.
For these holes are not holes. They are much more.
These holes run deeper than a man can fathom,
Run longer than any man can surely dig.
They are rock but lin'd with purest gold leaf.
Many miles they run, miles within and beyond.

In December, the pumpkins have dried so hard
Some folk carve a twisted, coiling shape within.
A spiral spinning from the centre to the edge.
As with poor man Jacks, they light candle within
And the coiled snake glows out into the night.
It is the poor or miserly who do this
For it sends out a call to The One Who Knows
"We have no gold. We have none of our own,
And, for the sake of heaven, we have none of yours."
And The One Who Knows will slither past that house.
The One Who Knows will never enter within.
But other houses will be softly explor'd
And the one who knows will take back all the gold
For all the gold belongs to The One Who Knows.

A brave bold knight came to the meadow of black
To seek for sweet fortune and glory and fame.
To seek for a woman to share in his bed.
For ale to sup, meat to chew, dragons to slay.
For wealth, for honour, for garter and glory.
For diamonds, for gold, for jewellèd rings and crowns.
He came upon a cottage hidden by briar.
Windows peeking out like eyes behind a fan
Held by a coy courtesan, with pink roses,
Honeysuckle, ivy and blackberry entwined.
In the window of this cottage sat a turnip,
Dried and wrinkl'd by the summer's desert heat.
Drawing close to study the old veg'table,
The knight saw, cut into its dusty brown skin,
The leather'd outline of a serpent fierce.
Tongue darting, teeth gnashing, body twisting long
Around its own centre. The blacken'd remains
Of an abandon'd candle sat behind this
Carvèd vision. A pool of wax and charr'd
Wick show'd this to be some ancient lantern.
The knight rais'd his hand, rapping hard upon the oak.
He listen'd, hearing nothing but a lonely bird
And the stuttering breeze shaking the morning leaves
And branches. He push'd at the old oaken door.

The cottage was dank and quiet darkness.
   A cloying sweet smell of dry rotten matter,
Mix'd with the foulest stench of spoiled meat,
Seep'd into his nostrils causing him to choke.
The knight stepp'd careful forward, squinting through greys,
Blacks, patches of colour, lines of yellowing
Light cast on edges, frames and floors. Lively eyes,
Train'd for battle, ambush, skirmish and sweet fray,
Darted up, down, to left, to right as he crept.

In the dim was a huge old table bedecked
   With sliming fruit and moulded bread on platters.
A buzz of flies danc'd and wheel'd as playing boys
About the rotted food, whilst a deeper cloud of
Insects swarm'd about a figure sitting down
At table, still waiting for the pudding dish.
The deepest stench of decaying flesh call'd out
To the knight's nose. But, undaunted, he stepp'd close.
This man had once been old. His hair was once white.
Now the flesh had dripp'd away. The bloodied skull
Grinn'd wide and delighted at the visitor brave.
The knight had stomp'd many a battlefield, had seen
And smelt the newly and the long past dead.
He knew that this fellow had sat there so long,
Perhaps almost half a year. The knight reach'd out for
A candle hid among the spoiling fruit.
With flint and breath and patient spark it burst in
Brighting flame. The Corpse smil'd, the fruit glow'd warm,
The flies danc'd faster, madden'd, curious, entranc'd.
Shadows march'd in time to the flicker and spit
Of the toiling flame.

The knight look'd about the orang'd walls,
His keen eye caught by a sight so strange.
Behind the corpse stood a door with lock
And bolt and bolt and lock and chain upon
Chain upon chain. Shut tight. Lock'd to th'world.
Not to be opened except by brace of keys.

The knight walk'd the house, candle aflame. He search'd
The pantry, the old man's chamber, he even
Look'd into the chimney but could not find hair
Nor hide of any key. With great reluctance
The knight walk'd back to the table, peering close
At the rotting man. It did not take him long
To find them, hanging from his belt, cover'd and
Coated in sloughs of dangled skin. The knight gripp'd
The iron ring, pulling it hard, ripping it from
The sticking flesh and leather thong holding it
To the breeches. In excitement and joy he
Tried the keys in locks, releasing bolts and chains
In a clattering clash of metal on floor.
The door stood naked, inviting, bidding him
To lift the latch, to enter, to come into
The darkness. And so he did. He took a breath.
His candle flame flicker'd. Hundreds of flames lick'd
Back at him. Reflections of fire on polish'd
Gold. More gold than the knight had ever even
Seen. Piles and piles of sweet sweet gold.
And, for an age, the knight stood still, marvelling.
All dreaming smiles and quiet snorts of joyous mirth.

As the sun sat high, the knight dug a deeping grave
To lay the rotted stranger down a'sleeping.
He clear'd and swept. Open'd the shutters wide and
Let the breeze without push the foulness within
From the dining table where death had sat still.

He lit a fire in the grate, watching the flames
Lick about the haunch of hart he had procur'd
From a hunter he had met on the road.
As he drifted to sleep he did not note the
Crickets cease, the owls grow dumb, or the foxes
Bite their tongues. If he had but glanc'd out of the
Window he would have seen a dozen flick'ring
Tiny spirals at the windows of all the
Other dwellings nearby. He would have seen more.
The long dark shape uncurling from the peak of
A distant hill. The black ridge rippling against
The star fleck'd sky, coiling from house unto house,
Wrapping its bulk around those that did not spark
With orange spiral lights. Ripping at the oak
Doors with yard long fangs, ignoring the screams and
Cries and the weeping relief as the beast swept
Away empty mouth'd. Had he open'd his eyes
He would have seen it slither along the path,
Sweeping with the fresh'ning breeze through the open
Doorway. Had he not been so tired he would
Have awoken as it whirlpool'd about the rooms,
Its dark scaléd hide brushing against the chair in
Which he snor'd, its spine level with the crown of
His head. The stacks of gold were behind lock'd door.
But The One Who Knows flar'd its angry nostrils.
The One Who Knows widen'd its eyes in a rage.
The One Who Knows roar'd a ruthless roar, tearing
The oak with its teeth like wet paper. At this, the
Knight did stir. The hart in his belly lurch'd wild.

He sprang to his feet, fumbling for his sword, but
Found his way block'd by the dark scal'd hide of
The fearsome Coyle. The tail by the knight flex'd
And rippl'd, turning, twisting and so swiftly
Embracing the blear-eyed knight that no shout nor
Cry escaped his lips. He was engulf'd, entrench'd
Deep within the spirals of the clenching tail.
But what of its head? Had the knight been able
To watch he would have seen the vast tongue flicking
Out, wrapping around coin and cup and figure
And candlestick and cruciform and ornate shield.
He would have seen all the gold he had smil'd at,
All the gold that had fill'd him with mirth and dreams
Of glory and castles and wenches and feasts.
Seen all of that wealth, all of those sweet riches
Vanish down the gullet of the greedsome beast.
But he did not see the Coyle's feast. He could
Not see the sweet gold swallow'd down the throat of
The One Who Knows. For The One Who Knows had bound
Him tightly in his scaled spiral twisting tail.
For all was black in the knight's dark world. His breath
So shallow, his sleep so deep, his heart so slow
In the cold cocoon of the clutching Coyle.

The knight awoke with such a frightsome jumping
That he thought his heart had ceas'd its drumming beat.
He was surpris'd to find himself alive.
He wriggl'd his toes, clench'd his fists, shook his head,
Took a deeping breath and blink'd open his eyes.
A shock of yellow and gold fill'd his vision.
All 'round ev'ry side, wall, ceiling and floor was
Gold. Gleaming gold. Glist'ning so loud he could hear
The bright sparkle, the royal roaring riches
Shouting forth their wealth. Their opulence tempting
Him to take, to grab, to grasp, to be the thief and run.

27

Run to the town, to the city walls.
Buy the King's palace from the King. Make him bow.
Buy the army from the Turk and make them fall
On their own swords and clear the Temple Mount.
Buy a princess fair or two, or a sweet score
Of maidens for him to wed and kiss and taste.
He sprang into action. Holding crown and bar,
Coin and necklace, bracelet and cup in his arms,
He stagger'd through the golden tunnel, slipping
On the polish'd, wet and slime-drench'd glist'ning floor.
Still clutching desp'rate to his ill-gotten gains
He flopp'd onto his back like a landed trout.
The tunnel slop'd steeply down and so the knight
Slipp'd into the bright depths of the Coyle's lair.
Until, with a cacophony of clatter,
And crash of metal on bone and flesh on stone
He came to a rest, ungainly, tangl'd tight
Within a cairn of stolen wealth hid from sight.
Hid from the cunning sight of The One Who Knows
In its sweet-fill'd pantry of most precious treats.
Try as he might the knight could not shift the weight
Of gold upon his frame. With each attempt he
Caus'd coin and bars to tumble, burying him
Deeper within the sparkling mound. He tried to
Cry out, but his mouth fill'd with trinkets and dust.
So the knight lay still. He did not move an inch.
He calm'd his breathing lest the rise and fall of
His chest caus'd more of the gold to tumble down
Upon him. He must have lain that way for an
Hour or more when he heard the familiar
Slither of scale on gold. The hiss of foulest breath.
The One Who Knows had come to take its sup.
Around the mound it curl'd, mouth drooling with deep
Desire for gilded treats to dance down its throat.

The Coyle rear'd its head, rising above the pile
Opening its mouth wide and biting down into
The treasure it crav'd so deep. It did not hear
The cry of pain, nor note the struggling form of
The knight, as he join'd the mass of coin and bar,
Of necklace, crown, ornament and sacred cross
In the warm, stinking maw of The One Who Knows.

The knight watched as the loot slid down
The gullet of the Coyle, slipping from sight
Into the dark red depths of gut and stomach.
But he could not move. The yard long fang skewered
His thigh right through, holding him dangling like old
Gristle wedg'd betwixt the ill-kept teeth of an
Ancient peasant. He held back his scream of pain,
Bending at the waist to grip the fang in a
Tight embrace lest he fall into the scarlet
Belly of the serpent. The vast forkèd tongue
Search'd for more morsels to swallow down.
Damp red leather flesh slopp'd against his face working
At pushing him from its tooth. Try as he could to resist
The knight found himself sliding down the long tooth.

Screaming loud as his wound left a hot trail of
Holly-berry gore on the gleaming iv'ry
Fang of The One Who Knows. As he slipp'd from the
Tip he reach'd to his belt and grasp'd at the hilt
Of his dagger. With a swiftness that belied his
Weaken'd state, he thrust the blade into the tongue
Before he could tumble down into the depths.
The Coyle let fly a roar of such ferocity
That blood flow'd sudden from the brave knight's ears
But still he clung to the thrashing tongue, wrapping
His arms and legs tight about the snaking form.
The Coyle thrash'd its head fast from side to side,
Up and down, but still he held rigid, clamp'd fast.
The knight squeez'd the tongue with his thighs ignoring
The burning pain that sear'd from the freshly bit
Hole, dripping with mingl'd blood, spit and venom.
A rumbling sounded from the depths below and
So he squeez'd again, tighter this time and yelp'd
With joy as he felt the serpent rise upwards.
Up and up, through tunnel and mud until a
Breeze could be felt 'gainst his tear-streak'd face.
The Coyle could fight it no more, its gorge arose.
The knight loos'd his blade and let the wave of gold
Effulgent sweep him from the maw onto the
Sweet purpling heath of the Black Meadow
Where he lay panting, gazing up at the Coyle
Gasping, lolling its wounded tongue, crying out
Into the dawn. The vast serpent wrapp'd itself
About a spiral cover'd stone and gaz'd

Down upon the beaten form of the brave knight.
So they sat, exhausted. One glaring upon
The other, until, with tail swishing behind,
The One Who Knows swept down into its golden
Lair leaving the knight to tend his poison'd limb.

In the days to come the knight found himself at
A local monastery. He had limp'd and
Crawl'd from the standing stone before finally
Collapsing in a ditch by the side of the
Road. He clos'd his eyes and resign'd himself
To the cold embrace of death. But when he woke
The warm sun shone bright through open window
And a kindly friar was tending to his leg.
As the days pass'd he regain'd his health and strength.
The poison, that he fear'd would cause his ending,
Appear'd to have done little harm. A lengthy sleep
Was all that The One Who Knows had dealt him.

And so after a month and sev'ral weeks had
Pass'd, he bid farewell to the kindly monks and
Went his way, seeking employment with any
Baron or King who would trust his strength or steel.

Within three months he was in the rich employ
Of a gen'rous merchant, guarding his goods from
Wicked bandits or crafty sneak-thieves who would
Stop at nothing to steal the finest silks or
Trinkets from this well-travell'd kindly master.

At the end of his first week the merchant call'd
The knight to his counting house. On ent'ring the
Room the knight found himself surrounded by neat
Stacks of gold coin, the merchant adding aloud
And writing down the profits gain'd that week.
The knight's new master look'd up, grinn'd so wide
That the knight was reminded of the vast maw
Of the slav'ring Coyle bearing down upon him.

"You have done well, oh knight, in your work for me,
I would like to reward you most generously.
Take five gold coins. Next week you shall have five more.
For your prowess with the sword, the fear you rais'd
I'th'heads of the bandits, sav'd me ten times
As much. I wish you to stay in my service.
Protect my goods, defend my name and warn all
Those who would dare abuse me to gain riches,
That they will gain nought but pain and injury."
The knight smil'd at these words and at the merchant's
Offer. It was gen'rous, though a paltry sum
Compar'd to the gold he had so nearly own'd.
The merchant grinn'd in return, counting out five
Gold coins, dropping them i'th' knight's open palm.
As shining metal hit flesh a great scream rent
The air. The skin on his palm bubbl'd, sizzling
Like gammon on a spit, or porridge boiling
In a cauldron. The knight's face, once handsome, turn'd
Garish red, pitted with gruesome open sores.
Within moments rancid egg yolk pool'd and dripp'd
From each crater, spreading across cheeks, down the
Nape of his neck, along his arms. Boil after
Boil, open welling sores, dripping with foul
Putrescence. The knight sank to the floor with a
Low whimper, screaming as his skin burst apart
With the slightest press, movement or shift of weight
The merchant gap'd in horror at this sorry
Sight. He stepp'd over the quivering form before
Running into the street calling "Physician!"
The golden coins peeled away from the knight's palm
Taking with it flesh, gristle and damaged skin.
As it slough'd onto the floor the knight's pain ceas'd.
On the wall, behind the body of the fell'd
Knight, the shadow of a serpent began to dance.

Waking sev'ral days later in the very
Same bed, tended by the very same kind monk.
His face and arms were bandag'd. He resmbl'd
A poor leper but was assur'd that his skin
Would recover in good time. The monk spoke truth.
And, within a month the knight sought employment.
But, on the day of payment, the affliction
Struck again, more painful this time, more grotesque
After inevitable recuperation
He asked the kind monk to bring him something gold,
To watch closely as it was plac'd in his palm.
The kind monk did as he was bidden to do
And look'd on in terror as the plague of boils spread
Over the poor knight's skin. He gasp'd with horror
As those boils pool'd pus and cross'd himself as the
Shadow of a vast serpent appear'd on the
Wall behind the stricken knight. The monk took the
Coin and flung it as far from him as he could.
He shook his head at the knight and told him that he
Could never touch gold or wealth ever again.
He must live his life in poverty or die
The victim of the bite of The One Who Knows.
The brave knight wept, tears stinging his ravag'd face.
He would ne'er touch gold again, nor feel its shine,
Nor feel the warmth it could bring, the tender touch
Of the bought wench, the comfort of the castle wall,
The strength of armour, the weight of blessed steel.
None of this could be his for the curse forbade
All gold. All wealth would destroy this poor
Brave knight for all gold belongs to
The One Who Knows.

The traveller lower'd his head and the pilgrims sat
Gazing at this poor man whose tale had so caught
Their tongues and stolen their hearts.
"What of the knight?" spake one.
The traveller lifted his head and smil'd,
The fire illuminated his pock-mark'd face,
Cast a shadow on the wall, not the shadow
Of the beaten man, but the shadow of a
Vast serpent, dancing, coiling and spiralling,
Turning great circles in the flickering light.

Ancient Tales

Legend of the White Horse

Legend of the White Horse

The Son of a Great Lord went out hunting one morning in the late spring. The heather sang to the dance of the bees. The gorse rippled in the breeze, its yellow flowers smiling out like little joyous suns amongst the dull thorns. The Son of the Great Lord looked across the Black Meadow at a clump of trees in the distance. He had been hunting a great old stag. This one had sired many younger stags that now ran merry hell across the moors, spreading deer over hill and dale like mould stains on a damp wall. The stag had clearly lumbered this way. The heather was trampled; branches of gorse were ripped and broken. Though its meat would be dry, its antlers would make a fine present for his father. He could picture them hanging above the Great Lord's impressive oak throne as he scoffed down the well stewed stag meat with the gravy from his platter.

The Son ran, keeping low, towards the copse. The sound of cracking twigs and the rustling of leaves were beyond the mere power of the wind. He dropped to the ground as the great old stag pushed through the brush towards him. The bow was in his hand, an arrow locked, string taut, ready to fly. As the stag broke cover, the arrow flew, planting itself deep into its chest. The stag dropped heavily without a sound. Moving stealthily forward, the Son dropped to his haunches before checking the stag was dead. Steam rose from the hide of the magnificent beast. The Son extracted the arrow. After wiping the gore off with his bare hands, he wiped the warm scarlet over his face.

It was time to take his prize home. He gripped the antlers and pulled hard. The corpse would not budge. He hacked two stout branches from a nearby tree and bound the animal to the two poles. Heaving the ends on to his shoulders, he tried to pull his prize home, but he barely moved an inch. His shoulders strained, his elbows locked, his arms screamed. His veins stuck out of his head – his eyes clamped shut, every muscle taut and tense. He shifted forward about half a foot. He opened his eyes, moaning at the pathetic progress he had made.

Standing in front of him was the epitome of equine beauty.

Sixteen hands high, with a hide as white as a fresh snowdrop, stood a beautiful white mare. Its eyes, as dark as jet, within its cloud white face, stared deep into the heart of the Son.

The lad asked, "Where have you sprung from?"

The mare gave a soft whinny before turning its back upon the young man. It stood there for a moment, white tail flicking in the breeze. The lad stood wondering, before a simple thought occurred to him.

"Help me with this," he said to the White Horse, "And I promise to care for you, forever."

The mare lowered its head and raised it again. They appeared to have an agreement. He raised the poles from the ground, fixing them in place to a length of rope around its belly. All the time he did this the creature did not stir. It did not move a leg, or shift its weight, it barely flicked an ear or swished a tail.

Once all was in place the Son tapped its behind and the two walked together across the heath, dragging the vast cadaver along the ground behind them.

The White Horse and the young man kept in step together. When the man stopped to take a swig of wine from his skin, the horse stopped too. When the horse stopped to lap at the water from a puddle the Son found himself stopping and waiting. This unison of movement continued all the way to the Great Hall.

There was great rejoicing when father saw the magnificent stag. It took four men, with much straining and puffing, to carry the stag to the butcher.

That night the White Horse stood in the stable whilst the Son, his father and mother, sisters, brothers and noblemen sat down to feast under the shadow of the enormous antlers. As he ate the stew, the young man felt a strange pang in his breast. He felt a pull, as though a rope, tied around his middle, was dragging him to the main doors. He staggered to his feet. The crowd grew silent and looked at him with anticipation.

"A toast," he cried, raising his goblet. "A toast to my father in his fiftieth year. May the luck of his ancestors be his. May many more antlers, more splendid than this, decorate his walls."

The crowd gave a cheer and the Lord thanked his son, proud tears starting his aging eyes. The Son raised his glass again before putting it down and making his way to the main doors without a backward glance, determined. The crowd didn't murmur at this, they assumed he had taken this moment to relieve himself. The hall quickly filled with idle chatter that faded as the door swung shut behind him and he approached the stables where she waited.

The White Horse gave a gentle neigh as he walked towards her. The other horses stood statue-like against the back wall of the stable, heads lowered, not one of them looking this way. The Son held out his hand to the horse, she took a tentative step forward and nuzzled his palm. The Son smiled. He stroked her soft warm hide before leading the white horse out into the moonlight. The night was warm, the silver light of the full moon cast a glorious aura around her majestic shape. The white horse lowered her head. The Son nodded, reached up and pulled himself onto her back. With his hands bound in the hair on her crest, he tapped her flanks with his heels and they rode out into the night.

These nocturnal adventures occurred every night for several months. He did not notice the quiet conversations between his mother and father or the shaking heads of the grooms. Every night he would visit the stable, the White Horse would come out into the dark and they would ride out onto the moor.

As the cold of autumn began to creep across the moor, his father called him into the great hall. Standing with him was an old man whom the Son recognised as the Squire of a neighbouring house. The Squire's hands tightly gripped the arms of a young girl. The girl looked to the floor. The Squire's grip tightened. The girl looked up and on the pressure from another squeeze, forced a tiny smile.

"This girl is to be yours," the Lord commanded. "Your union will cement the fortunes of our two great families."

The Son stood silent for a moment. He and the girl eyed each other nervously.

"What do you say?" The Lord frowned. "This is a great day for all of us."

The Squire leant and whispered something into his daughter's ear. She nodded, but a single tear escaped from the corner of her eye.

Her voice quavering, she recited, "I am yours good sir. I will be a good wife to you and ensure both our family's future success."

The Son smiled at her. He nodded to his father. He nodded at the squire. Remaining silent, he turned his back upon them before walking through the main entrance and out to the stable.

He rode upon his White Horse out onto the meadow. He did not direct the mare, instead he let her roam where she wished. The White Horse galloped at speed and with apparent purpose. She left the well-trodden path, taking him across unfamiliar territory, further and further away from his home.

A mist rose upon the heather. Soft tiny cobwebs of cloud, resting amongst the purple flowers, grew dense until they hid the hooves and cannons of his ride. Soon the mist was so deep he could not see his own feet. As the ground dipped away, the mist enveloped them entirely. Still the mare trotted forward with absolute certainty, never stumbling, moving ever forward.

The air grew warmer and the Son could hear the distant sounds of drums and singing. The mist began to clear, revealing a field full of horses standing in a circle. The white mare lowered her head, signalling the Son to dismount. She trotted calmly over to the circle and stood with them, still waiting as the music from the surrounding mist grew ever louder.

As the beat increased in intensity, the horses began to move. They trotted in time towards the centre until their heads touched. They stepped backwards, their feet poring at the heather. Their movements became rhythmic. As the beat increased faster, their movements became fluid and seemed to blur. Shapes began to change. The Son blinked. The horses now seemed to be raising themselves onto their hind legs as one. Their large bodies shrinking, thinning. Hooves flattened. Chests imploded. Hair shed. The music stopped, the movement slowed and there, standing in a circle, breathless, was a crowd of naked men and women. Eyes bright and smiles wide. They sang out into the night: a chant of beauty and love. The circle widened and split revealing in its centre a beautiful maiden with a shock of white blonde hair upon her head. She looked up at the Son. She stepped towards him. The circle closed. The music from the mist began and the dance resumed. The woman with the white hair drew close to the Son. He held out his hand, meaning to stop her. Fear hammered at his chest. She stepped closer and nuzzled his palm. The Son's eyes widened. She shivered. He removed his coat and placed it around her shoulders. She smiled and took his hand, leading him through the mist with absolute certainty, back to his home.

The Lord was waiting at the gate as they approached late the next morning.

"You insulted our guests," he growled.

"I could not marry that girl," the Son smiled.

The Lord's eyes glinted red. "And why is that?"

"He had already made promise to me," whispered the White-Haired Girl.

"And who are you?"

"She is mine," stated the Son. "And I am hers."

The Lord laughed, "Where did you find this stray?"

"She was on the moor."

"Foraging was she? A common peasant by the looks of her. She does not even wear clothes that fit." The Lord laughed again, pulling her coat open.

The White-Haired Girl pulled it shut and held it tight.

The Lord shook his head. He hissed in his son's ear, "You have had your final dalliance, boy. You bring this woman here, this villein child, for what? You think she will sit at your right hand? Is she from a noble family?"

"I love her, father."

"You do not know her. You have not spent time seeking out love. Which is why I have found you a mate. You spent more time with that wretched mare..." He stopped, eying the White-Haired Girl closely. "So that was why you were so keen to go out riding every day. This one had you bewitched, eh? Riding out to her hovel every evening?"

"She is no peasant, sir."

"Then what is she?"

The Son clamped his mouth tight.

But the White-Haired Girl, she was of nature and as such, blunt and truthful to a fault. "I am his wretched mare, sir. I took him from his home tonight to a place where he watched me dance and I became what you see now. He has already made promise to me and that promise cannot be broken."

The Lord stood in shocked silence at this. The Son shook his head slowly, as the White-Haired Girl stared defiantly at his father.

The Lord found his voice. "This is utter devilry. My poor son, bewitched. My poor son." Tears filled his eyes and he pulled the boy into a tight embrace. "I have you, boy. You are free from her vice."

"She is no witch," whispered the Son, tearing himself away from his father's arms.

The Lord stepped back and stated, calmly, "I understand, son. You cannot be free from her spell at the clap of hands. This will take time and the ministrations of holy men."

At a signal from the Lord, two guards stepped from the shadows.

"Do not lay hands upon her!" The Son lunged forward. The Lord grabbed his arm and, as he struggled against his father's grip, the guards took the White-Haired Girl from him.

For many nights the Son woke to the sounds of his beloved screaming as they sought out her mark. As they pricked her with needles. She too lay awake in the day listening to the prayers about his bed, the chants and the hymns and *his* screams as they burnt the witchery from him. He suffered a cycle of branding, healing and prayer. But still he would not relent. He refused to eat and began to waste away. The white-haired girl shivered quietly in her cellar. The son shivered silently in his bed.

In the great hall the Lord and his priests conferred. The only way for his Son to be free from this enchantment was for the witch to die. For with her death, the spell would break. Her power over him would cease.

In the courtyard, outside the great hall, preparations were made, wood gathered, a pyre built with a tall stake standing upright in the centre.

The priests said their prayers around the pyre as a crowd gathered. The Son crept to his chamber window, his hand pressed against the pane. A low howl of anguish escaped his lips as he watched the two guards bring the White-Haired Girl out of the cellar towards the pyre. As she was tied to the stake, a priest asked if she had any final words to speak. She looked up at the bedroom window, her distant face seeming to nuzzle at his palm.

"He has already made promise to me. And that promise cannot be broken."

The priest shook his head, gesturing for the pyre to be lit. The crowd began to stamp their feet and clap their hands, singing out an angry hymn. As the flames licked around the base of the fire, the volume increased.

The Son turned from the window. He looked for the guard standing at the door and saw that he had moved to look through the other window, leaving the door unprotected. As the song reached the second verse and the crowd grew louder, the Son was already halfway down the stairs, his guard in swift pursuit.

The rhythm of the hymn increased, the flames licked higher. The White-Haired Girl swayed against her bonds. Those who saw her, swore that she was swaying in time to the rhythm of the hymn. As the third verse began, the Son was in the courtyard. He could see the top of his beloved's head nodding in time to the violence of the holy song and the rhythm of the stamping feet and clapping hands that accompanied it. He ran at the flames, crying out as the burning logs singed at his feet as he leaped towards the stake. But the crowd sang on, enchanted by the power of the spell that they were weaving, held together by this unity of hatred and fear. The rhythms of their anger giving power to their volume, to their percussion, to their wretched song.

The smoke filled the square. The people sang, feet stamping, hands clapping.

And, in the centre of the flames, two people danced together. The heat growing, the volume increasing, the shapes changing.

Then, with a flurry of cinder and ash, a beautiful white mare and a majestic black stallion burst from the centre of the flames and galloped out of the courtyard and into the warm October mists.

Heather and Bramble

The Blackberry Ghost

The Blackberry Ghost

It is a tradition to send your child out to pick blackberries alone on the first night of September. All the villagers know the stories - they started them.

If you want your family to have good luck and good jam then this is the best night for a blackberry harvest. The children go prepared with basket, gloves and crucifix. The Blackberry Ghost is out that night. The Blackberry ghost knows where the best brambles will be found.

This tale concerns the story of a child who had no parents. He lived in an old shed by the side of a farm. The farmer took him in when both his parents disappeared into the mist. The child played alone. He worked the farmer's field for a hunk of bread and a glass of milk every day. This child thought that if he were to gather blackberries with the rest of the children he might gain some friends. The other children did not talk to him. It was considered bad luck to converse with anyone whose parents had been swallowed by the meadow fog.

On the first night of September the boy borrowed a basket from the farmer. The bramble branches swayed in the soft breeze. He squinted through the dusk. There was a slight path through the blackberry that looked most promising. Other children were entering the field, their parents waving them on. Wishes of good luck could be heard echoing over the vast field of bramble. Suddenly he felt a violent shove. He found himself on the cold ground, his elbows scraped. He saw, disappearing down the path he had found, a tall gangly lad with messy brown hair. The boy sat up, tears began to well in his eyes. Why would someone be so cruel?

He had never harmed anyone. All he ever did was sit alone in a shed by the side of the farm. A shaft of moonlight broke through the clouds. Its beam settled on a patch of bramble in front of him. Looking closely, he could see a small opening in the blackberry. He crawled forward on his hands and knees, ignoring the pain from his tumble. Even in the dim light of dusk it was clear that this opening continued on into a tunnel of thorns. The boy grinned, grabbed his basket and made his way into the blackberry field.

He crawled for hours, pushing the basket along in front of him. Occasionally he would happen upon a shrivelled or desiccated berry which he would pick, examine and discard. He wrinkled his nose in frustration. He considered turning back but there was no room to rotate. Resolved, he crawled further, noticing that the tunnel of thorns was becoming narrower. His basket remained empty. It felt as though hours had passed. Exhausted, he collapsed onto his front. Sobs ripped from his throat. He could hear the laughter of children in the distance.

He lay there for some time. After a little while he heard a pattering sound. Slowly raising his head he saw a blackberry drop into the basket from above. He stared. Another dropped in. He crawled forward to look over the rim of the basket. There was another. Blackberry after blackberry plopped into the basket. And these weren't dry old husks. These weren't small and pathetic. These were the most delicious, succulent blackberries anyone had ever seen. The boy laughed aloud, watching in wonder as the basket began to fill. He craned his neck to see where they came from. He rolled onto his back. He peered up through the mess of bramble. A face was smiling down at him. The shimmering, silvery, see-through face of a young boy, about his age. The ghost opened its misty hand over the blackberry basket. From between its fingers fell the fruit of the bramble. Soon the basket was overflowing. The ghost boy grinned and faded away. The boy stayed where he was for several moments, his mouth gaping open. Once recovered, he continued to push the basket forward through the tunnel of thorns.

Within minutes he found himself in a large open space. The lad with messy brown hair was staring at him as he emerged. The boy stretched. The gangly lad gazed enviously at his basket. His own was a quarter full. The quality was mediocre. The boy grinned. He nodded at his own basket, allowing the lad to take a blackberry from the top. The gangly lad smiled and the boy's heart filled with joy. But the gangly lad did not take a blackberry. Instead he snatched the basket and pushed the boy to the ground. He sneered his thanks, stuffed his grubby fingers into the pile of fruit and scooped a handful into his mouth, chewing voraciously. Dark red and purple juice ran down his chin. He scooped up another handful. His mouth worked greedily at the juicy harvest. He grinned and chewed. Scooped again. He chewed and grinned. As the boy watched through his tears, he saw the gangly lad's eyes suddenly become very wide. A short, muffled whimper escaped from between his closed lips. Even in the dark the boy could see the blood pouring out from between his teeth. The lad opened his mouth wide, choking. A bramble leaf poked out. He retched. Grabbing the leaf between his fingers he pulled frantically. A trail of bramble emerged from his mouth. It tore at his lips. It tore at the insides of his cheeks. He slowed his action, knowing that the faster he went the more damage it would do. The boy watched in horror as a long trail of blood-soaked bramble piled at the gangly lad's feet. The bully sank to his knees. He pushed the basket towards the boy. The boy took it and popped a blackberry nervously into his mouth. The blackberry exploded between his teeth, releasing a beautiful sweetness. He patted the gangly boy on the head, turned and skipped down the path to share his harvest with the farmer.

Heather and Bramble

A Voice from the Heather

A Voice from the Heather

When Charlie Ellerton was nine, his mother told him a story.

They had been out to the village that day when an old woman, wrinkled beyond repair, thrust a crudely bound bunch of heather into his tiny hands.

Her eyes shone black lightning into his and she whispered, "Lucky heather. Listen." She grabbed him by the wrist. "Listen!" She waggled a stalk next to her ear before thrusting it next to her own. "Listen," she rasped.

Mother intervened. She gave the old woman two pennies and thanked her for the heather. The old woman tried to give the money back.

"It is a gift," she insisted. "Listen."

Mother Ellerton told the old woman that they were grateful but that they had to get home. She pulled Charlie away, gripping his hand tightly all the way home.

That night as they sat around the table for supper Charlie looked up at his Mother.

"Why did the old lady say 'Listen' Ma?"

Mother was silent as she warmed the soup. She did not speak as Charlie and his father swallowed it down with noisy slurps. It was only once the dishes were washed and drying on the rack that she told Charlie the story.

"As long as anyone can remember," she said. *"People have talked about the voice in the heather. My mother told me this story and my grandmother told it to her.*

I don't know how far it goes back. There was a farmer."

"There is always a farmer in these stories," smiled Father.

"There was a farmer," she continued with barely a glance at her husband. *"He owned three fields. On one he grew wheat, on the second, grass for sheep to graze, but on the third nothing would grow but heather. He ploughed it and sowed barley upon it, but heather grew. He put down lime, but heather grew. Last of all he waited until it was dry and put flame to it. Watched it burn and smoke and smoulder to black. The field sat dead. The heather ash drifted in the wind. The rain fell, turning the black ash to a dark tar. The farmer tilled the soil, ripping up the old roots, planting potatoes, the hardiest crop he could find. It was not a crop that would bring wealth, but it would be sure to bring in more money than any heather would.*

He glanced out of the window one balmy spring morning and saw the inevitable haze of green on the blackened ground. As the days went on the purple pink flowers appeared and the farmer shrugged with defeat. Heather. His field was just a blasted heath crammed to bursting with blasted heather. No potatoes, no barley, no grazing grass. Only heather would grow on this benighted field.

The heather grew in abundance. It was a beautiful sight to behold. The gentry and ladies of leisure, walking in the fields for recreation, stopped on the brow of the hill overlooking the field and gazed down at the beautiful sight. Word spread. A landscape painter, famous for his series of paintings known as 'The Stone Steps', paid the farmer for lodgings in one of the outhouses, so he could capture the beauty of the heather across the seasons. Several artists followed suit and for a few years the field of heather reaped some sort of reward for the farmer. Gradually the interest, at least the kind that would bring any kind of wealth, dried up and the field of heather became an irritation once more.

It was on a hot August afternoon, as he was harvesting in the wheat field, that he saw three ladies clad in long skirts and headscarves walking towards him. They had something of the Romany about them and, when they spoke, in that exotic lilt, he knew that they were clearly Gypsies and probably the cunning women of their tribe.

'Your heather is fine,' one of them said. 'May we take some cuttings to sell?'

The farmer felt he must oblige, for the curse of a thwarted cunning woman was not one that could be shaken off with three Hail Marys and a dab of prayer. He watched them closely as they went about their business, cutting and trimming the choicest sprigs for their trade.

'This one is very good,' announced the first. 'Listen to its voice!'

The other two skipped forward and leaned in to study the sprig with heads cocked towards it.

'It shrills loud,' confirmed the second.

'It sings,' added the third with a giggle of delight.

The first pointed to a clump of bright purple in the centre of the field. The farmer watched, fascinated, as they stripped the patch bare.

'It's deafening,' called the first as though screaming above a cacophony.

'What did you say? It's so loud,' shouted the second.

The farmer watched as they walked past with their baskets full to overflowing.

'Thank you sir,' the three cunning women said in unison.

His curiosity got the better of him and he found himself asking them, 'What can you hear?'

'The cry of the purple,' said the first.

'The whisper of the pink,' said the second.

'The question of the stalk,' said the third.

The farmer frowned, aside from the wind in the tall grass and the song of a distant thrush, he could hear nothing at all. He told them this and they smiled.

'This is a fine crop,' said the first.

'The best we have seen,' nodded the second.

'And you have been most helpful and kind,' said the third.

'Listen,' said the first, holding her basket close to the farmer's face.

'Listen,' said the second, holding her basket close to the farmer's left ear.

'Listen,' said the third, holding her basket close to the farmer's right ear.

The farmer listened. Aside from the wind rattling the fences, the grass rustling, the call of the thrush and its mate singing in answer, he could hear nothing at all. He told them this and they smiled.

'You will hear,' said the first.

'You shall hear,' said the second.

'You can hear,' said the third.

The first took his hand, pulling it deep into the heather in her basket. The second placed a garland of heather upon his head. The third cut her finger *before dripping three drops of crimson into his left and right ear.*

The farmer heard a buzzing in his head, a hush and finally an almost silent whisper. He swooned. All was darkness.

When he woke it was night. The three cunning women were long gone. He was lying in the centre of the field of heather, his head bedecked with a heather crown and his ears flecked with dried Romany blood. He lay there for a while listening to the breeze, the birds and the whisper. The whisper in his ears.

The farmer returned to his house. The whispering grew fainter as he moved away from the heather, becoming indistinct but, just as with the distant sound of waves breaking against the shore, although he could no longer hear them he knew they were there.

For weeks he worked hard on the other fields. He was deliberately avoiding the heather. When he walked close he could hear a whisper but he couldn't make out any words.

He had a troublesome ewe that escaped from its field. He followed it across the wheat-field onto the road and paused, watching as it leapt a low hedge and ran into the heather field. The ewe made its way into the centre of the field and stood, looking at him. The farmer stayed in the road. The whispering was more distinct, he thought he could make out a word repeated over and over. The ewe blinked its eyes. If she could have beckoned she would have. The farmer moved to the hedge line and called the ewe to him. The ewe blinked and blinked but did not move. The farmer sighed and opened the gate.

'More,' whispered the heather.

The farmer walked a few paces into the field.

'More,' said the heather.

The farmer walked towards the ewe. It did not budge.

'More,' called the heather.

He was by the ewe now. He bent and lifted it onto his shoulders.

'More,' shouted the heather.

He made his way back to the gate.

'More,' sang the heather. 'More. More.'

In the house, even with the windows shut and the curtains drawn, he could still hear the voice from the heather. As his wife spoke to him of the children and of the gossip from the village, he could still hear the voice from the heather. As he wrapped the pillow around his head and his wife snored gently in the bed next to him, he could still hear the voice from the heather.

'More,' it said.

'More of what?' he wondered.

'More,' it said.

The whispering grew more irritating to the poor farmer. He was losing sleep. Was he losing his mind? He walked to the heather field, wondering whether burning it would cease the whispering, but knowing that burning would only bring it back more healthy and strong. Though it could quieten it for a short while. He patted his pocket to check the flint and steel was still there. Just in case. The whispering became more distinct.

'More,' the heather sang. 'Heather not wheat. Heather not sheep.'

'Heather not wheat? Heather not sheep?' he cried. 'What of my livelihood?'

'Only heather,' came the song. 'Only heather to bring success, to bring joy.'

'I shall burn the heather!'

'Yes,' sang the heather. 'Burn the heather, let it glow bright, come back stronger, let the flame lick the wheat and grass, let the heather embrace all your land.'

The song grew louder and louder, repeating and repeating. The farmer clamped his hands over his ears. The words of the heather pried at his fingers, slipping beneath the skin of his palms, pulling them away from the sides of his head. He fought to keep the noise out, but it crept through every crack of skin, every line of palm, pushing his hands further and further from his head until they hung limp and defeated by his sides.

'Let the heather embrace your land,' sang the purple.

'Let the heather embrace your land,' sang the pink.

'Let the heather embrace your land,' sang the mauve.

The voices joined in harmony. The farmer flicked the flint, letting the spark become a smoulder, the smoulder become smoke, the smoke become a flame and the flame become a blaze. The chorus did not end. The smoke only seemed to amplify it. The more the flame and smoke billowed, the louder the chorus grew. The farmer ripped up a flaming piece of heather, opened the gate to the wheat-field and flung the blazing branch into the drying crop. The flames licked greedily at the wheat, chasing the farmer to the next gate – to the sheep field. The grass, dried by sun and drought, welcomed the fire. The sheep bleated fearfully as the farmer lead them to the barn. The flames licked hungrily at the three fields, never stopping, always growing. Before too long, the blaze spread to the barns and the house. The farmer and his family ran to the summit of a nearby hill where they stood and watched as the smoke and fire engulfed the farm.

'What have you done?' cried the farmer's wife.

'I have let the heather embrace the land,' answered the farmer, smiling a warm smile.

The smoke billowed into the sky. The family breathed the grey cloud deep into their lungs. It drifted around their heads, into their nostrils and probed deep within their ears.

'A tower now,' it sang. 'A tower to the heather.'

The farmer asked his wife and children, 'Do you hear its song?'

They inhaled the warm fog, nodding their reply, eyes dull, but mouths smiling, as they sang, 'A tower now, a tower to the heather.'

The family watched silently, as the fields blazed and their house burnt to a blackened husk.

The farmer and his children built a shelter that overlooked the farm. They drank from a spring and slaughtered the oldest ewe – smoking the flesh they did not consume in the first week. Once the stones of the house cooled, the family began to dismantle the building, using the stones to construct a wide circle. Without speaking to each other or communicating what it was they wished to achieve, they created a round tower of blackened stone with three floors, a *chimney running up the centre and stairs running in a spiral around it to each floor. Once it was completed they piled earth up the outside, all the way to the very top. Once it was finished, save for the tiny windows that let in a modicum of air and light, the tower, built from the remains of the farmhouse and barns resembled a tall thin mound. By the following summer it and the surrounding fields were covered in heather.*

The farmer and his family were inundated with visitors. People came to see the strange heather tower but they stayed for the advice and the words they heard. The farmer and his family made more money from the service they provided to these pilgrims in one week than they ever managed in a year.

The sheep roamed free.

People would buy heather and ask what the future held. Should they marry this gentleman? Should they invest in that property? Should they move to the Americas? Should they start that business? The farmer or anyone from the family, (for all were established and natural augurs now, from the youngest child to the farmer and his wife), would pluck a piece of heather, and throw it in a flame from the fire at the base of the tower. They would inhale the smoke and let out their answer in their first exhalation.

'Do not marry. He is a cad and a bounder.'

'The property will thrive.'

'The Americas will serve you well.'

'Your business will fail. Abandon all thoughts of it at once and become a schoolmaster. That is the best path out of failure.'

Even the most sceptical were satisfied. The prophecies were always true and helpful. Those that did not heed them met with the predicted misfortune and those that did lived lives of happiness and comfort.

Each visitor was given a sprig of heather to plant near their home for they must "Let the heather embrace the land."

The farmer and his wife grew old. They lived well and comfortably. Their children did not marry but stayed together in the tower, giving advice and counsel to all who sought it.

When the farmer died the children took his body out to the field where they lay it on a pyre of dried heather. They watched and sang as the fields burnt. They repeated this two years later with the body of their mother and in later years as each of them succumbed to the ravages of age. The youngest continued to offer advice and on the day of his own death walked into the centre of the field with a lit torch. As he breathed his last breath the torch dropped from his hand the heather turned black again.

The smoke billowed across the land. It was said that wherever it touched, that patch of land would sprout heather. And, if you leaned close to listen, you could hear the heather whispering alongside the clear and distinct voices of the farmer and his family."

Charlie's mother stopped and took a sip of tea. Charlie leaned forward.

"Can you really hear voices in the heather, mother?"

His mother smiled. "Some believe it. In these parts it seems that many do."

Charlie was silent. After kissing his slumbering father on the cheek, his mother ushered him off to bed.

It is worth mentioning that Charlie was something of a mischievous soul. Where one person would skirt a puddle to avoid getting wet, Charlie would jump and splash. Where another would stand aside as a priest in a long cassock strolled past, Charlie would step forward to stamp on the trailing hem, causing the priest to stumble back, or, even better in Charlie's mind, causing the priest to curse a blue storm. So Charlie was always on the lookout for mischief and so it was, as he left the room to amble up to bed, that the seed of an idea was sown. As he pulled off his clothes and popped his head out of the hole in his nightshirt, that seed began to germinate. When he had burrowed beneath the sheets and said his prayers with mother, that idea began to flower. The next morning it bore fruit ready for the plucking.

Just a few hundred yards from their house was a field of heather, very similar to the one in mother's marvellous tale. Charlie's eyes glinted as he scanned the fence line. There was a clump of heather, just near the path, that was tall enough to hide inside. Charlie found an opening, cleared a path and made himself comfortable.

*

Elizabeth Tinker had no friends. She was a lonely child who spent her school days in the corner of the

71

classroom and the summers in her room looking out at the world. The problem was that Elizabeth thought that she was ugly. She balked at mirrors. She wore her hair long in curtains on either side of her face so that only the eagle-eyed could see her pretty nose or chin. Her mother would try to tie her hair back or hold it inside a pretty bonnet but, as soon as her back was turned, Elizabeth would undo the ties or throw off the bonnet and return to her hidden state. She had felt this way for as long as she remembered. When children of her age tried to talk to her she would shy away and give no answer. If they asked her to play she would retreat to the corner. Before long, they stopped asking.

Elizabeth crept down the path. Her mother had asked her to pick some blackberries for a pie she was making. Elizabeth was returning home, her head down, her hair hiding her face, and her basket pulled up to her chest, when she heard the whisper.

"Elizabeth."

She whirled around and could see no one.

"Elizabeth."

She called out, "Who's there?"

"Elizabeth Tinker."

She peered about. The voice seemed to be coming from the heather itself.

"You are ugly," whispered the voice.

She sobbed in surprise, "Wh-who is that?" She could see no one.

"You are foul."

"I know."

"You know?" the whisper chuckled. "Do you know what makes you most ugly? Do you know your foulest feature?"

Elizabeth stared about wildly.

The whisper continued. "Cut it off. Go home and cut it off. Everyone laughs at your hair. Cut it off. 'Curtains' they call you. 'Curtains'. Cut it off."

"Cut it off?"

"Cut it off. I, the heather, demand it."

Charlie smiled as Elizabeth Tinker ran to her house in floods of tears. There was something especially pleasing about making a girl cry – especially one as pathetic and weak as Elizabeth Tinker.

The next day as Charlie made his way to the heather for another ounce of mischief he saw a vision approaching him. Head held high, a gorgeous little nose, perfect teeth, full red lips and hair cut in a sweet style that bobbed about her ears. He could not fathom who she was or why he had not seen her before. He gasped as she passed and she smiled. The smile turned him red from his toes all the way to his crown. He turned to follow her departure. Approaching her was a young man, Tom, the blacksmith's son. He grinned at this beauty and asked her name, gasping in delight when he heard;

"Lizzie Tinker."

Charlie watched, amazed, as this girl, freed from her own prison of hair, spoke with confidence to the ogling Tom, before walking away from her home and out into the meadow to pick blackberries.

*

Charlie sniggered as he saw the priest approaching. Everybody knew about his outrageous flirtations with the milkmaid. People whispered behind their hands or spoke about it quietly, around the dinner table, in front of their uncomprehending children. Charlie, however, had comprehended. If there was a relationship going on between these two then it was considered "immoral", "disgusting", "hypocritical" and "beyond the pale", words and phrases that Charlie considered exotic and, for his current purposes, very useful.

Father Timothy battled with his shame. Meg was beautiful and could never be his. His hand touched her lips when he fed her the communion bread. When she shook his hand to compliment him on the sermon, they held on too long. Had people noticed their furtive looks, the little smiles? He felt sure they had. He felt his love for her was as clear as the moon on a cloudless night. The confessional had been where they had confessed their love for one another through the grill. They had shared soft words. Their love felt pure and good, but it could not be. It must not be, for he was wedded to the church. He could not give in to base, carnal desires. But this was not base and carnal. Certainly, he felt stirrings of lust when he gazed upon her, but it was her companionship that he craved. It was her by his side. Once, he had gone to kiss her, he hadn't meant to, she had moved close to him and he had moved his head forward, but, as she ducked her head demurely, he had pecked her on the nose. They had laughed at that. She turned and ran. As he watched her depart he felt an unbearable sadness for that one kiss was all that they could share. It was all that they could ever have.

His thoughts were interrupted by a sound to his left. A whispered snigger. He turned his head.

"Father Timothy," whispered a voice from the heather.

He frowned and looked towards the bush.

"Father Timothy," whispered the voice again.

"Who's there?"

"You are beyond the pale."

"What?"

"You are an immoral hypocrite."

"Who is that? Show yourself!"

"You preach chastity and purity and yet you gallivant off with a common milkmaid?"

Father Timothy looked behind him to check no-one was listening. "I do not know who you are but that is a lie. I have nothing but the utmost respect for Meg."

"You kissed her."

"I did not."

"On the nose."

"Oh. Well, that was a mistake. How did you…"

"The heather sees all."

"Oh."

"The heather knows all."

"Well, that was a mistake."

"Of course it was. You were aiming for her mouth."

"It will not happen again. Although I am a priest, I am a man. Although I serve God and the church, I am human. I err and stray like a lost sheep. But it will not happen again."

"Liar."

"What?"

"You love her."

"I…"

"Will you lie to the heather as you lie to yourself? Tell the heather you do not love her. Tell yourself that you do not love her. Lie."

"I do not… I cannot love her."

"That is not the same. You lie to yourself. Lying is a sin."

"I cannot say it."

"Then you lie and you will burn in hell and you will take her with you in your sin."

"I cannot say it."

"You love her."

"I…"

"Say it."

"I love…"

"Say it! Say her name! Say it!" The voice from the heather was growing in excitement and volume.

Father Timothy looked all around and whispered, "I love her."

"Who?"

"Meg Talchester."

"Put it together."

"What?"

"Say it all."

"I love Meg Talchester."

"You love Meg Talchester?"

"Yes."

"Did you just say you love Meg Talchester?"

"I did. I love Meg Talchester."

"You are an immoral disgrace."

"I don't care. Oh thank you!" The priest shouted, "I love Meg Talchester!"

"You are a disgrace to the church."

"Yes I am," grinned Father Timothy with happy realisation. "I am a disgrace!"

"You must cast off your cassock and leave the church. You must do it at once."

"Yes. Yes! Yes! You are right. Thank you."

Father Timothy skipped to the church. Charlie giggled in delight.

The service on the following Sunday was remembered for years to come. The congregation entered the empty church to gather in their usual places. Father Timothy walked up the aisle in breeches and shirt followed by a stern looking bishop in all of his fine robes and stole. At a nod from the bishop, Father Timothy gave an electrifying sermon about lying and consequences. He told the congregation how he was blessed to find the love of a good woman and that he could no longer lead them. He held out his hand to Meg, who was sitting, eyes shining with tears, in the third pew. She rose unsteadily to her feet and walked slowly towards Timothy. Their hands touched and he pulled her into an embrace. As they kissed in the centre of the church, the sun broke from behind a cloud and a shaft of warm yellow shone through the stained glass crucifix illuminating the couple in a pure and holy light. The congregation rose as one and cheered.

As the bishop spoke in dull and stern tones of standards, traditions, rules and replacements, Charlie wondered at the consequences of his mischief. Of how a bullied girl flowered into a confident young woman. He looked over at Lizzie Tinker laughing with two friends in the back pew. His intention had been unkind but the result did not reflect that unkindness. And now, looking at the former priest, sitting in the front row with Meg's head resting on his shoulder, both of them beaming serenely, how did his bullying words lead to this? Was he, Charlie Ellerton, puller of hair, tripper of feet and maker of mischief unwittingly a force for good?

*

Ben Tranter was not a happy man. His wife was unwell. The pox that had taken her father was deep on her skin and no ointment nor medicine would cure the malaise. Her breathing was growing weaker and she would not take food, she could barely cope with water. He walked the path from the dairy to his house past the field of heather. Sarah loved the heather, he thought, perhaps a sprig or two would raise her spirits. Raised spirits themselves could give her the strength to fight on. To keep going. Ben leant forward. As his fingers grasped at the heather he heard a voice.

"Ben Tranter," a high pitched voice whispered. "Ben Tranter."

"Who is it?" Ben searched about, trying to pinpoint the source. It appeared to be coming from directly in front of him, from the heather itself.

"Ben Tranter," said the heather. "The answer you seek is in the well."

"Who is it?"

"The well. Go to the old well."

"What is in the well?"

"Climb down the well. Gather water from the left side in an old tin cup, bring that up. Use it and the answer will be found."

Ben Tranter backed away from the heather. The old well? A voice in the heather? It was worth a try. After all, he had little left to lose.

Charlie giggled as he watched Ben hurrying into his house with the jug of milk. He laughed as he saw Ben emerge a few minutes later armed with rope and a tin cup. He guffawed as he watched Ben attach the rope to axle and climb down into the depths of the well. His laughter ceased as Ben emerged holding the tin cup firmly in one hand and holding onto the rope with the other. He stared in astonishment as Ben, who had clearly taken everything to heart, now walked to the house, abandoning the rope, but carrying the tin cup with the reverence that an altar boy saves for the crucifix.

His astonishment turned to a strange mix of dismay and joy when, a week later, he saw Mrs Tranter at the window, a scarred but healing face smiling out at him. The week after this she was in her garden and the week after that, sitting and chatting amiably with her neighbours in the fifth pew in the church, while the new vicar walked up the aisle. Everyone missed Father Timothy, his sermons were vibrant and fun. There was nothing fun about Father Thomas. He was tedious and lacked the spark of life that Timothy had in spades.

Charlie considered the causes of the good fortune of those he had counselled. Either he was imbued with some blessed power or something else was using him for its own ends. If either of these ideas were true then where was the fun in causing mischief? What was the point if beautiful chaos wasn't caused? If his mischief inevitably led to order, then why put in the effort? If he insulted them and they took his words to heart and acted on them, good fortune would visit them. If he deliberately led them down the wrong path, they would inevitably find an even better path than the first they were on. So Charlie resolved to not visit the heather again. He would not be the slave to some invisible force.

The morning after he had made this decision Charlie awoke to find himself in the heather.

He remembered settling down to sleep in his own bed and a series of restless dreams. In the first he had left his bedroom and house and laid down in the heather. In the second, as the tavern had emptied, he had poured vitriol at Patrick the Tanner informing him that he was a hopeless husband, more in love with his drink than his own wife. He had whispered curses at Andrew the blacksmith for his cruel treatment of his children, telling him that he must take himself to the lake and visit the village at its watery base, if they were to be free from his tyranny. He had sung a song to Mary Feltham of how a maid did not have to grow to be a wife but could strive to be more. But all of these were dreams, nothing more.

Except, as he lay blinking in the morning light, he knew they were real. Patrick was standing outside his house emptying bottle after bottle of hissing spirits into the gutter. Andrew the Blacksmith's wife and children were out of the house half-heartedly shouting for their husband and father. Mary Fentham was sitting by her window studying a book of scientific theory. When

80

Lizzie Tinker and her two friends approached Mary to ask if she would like to prepare for the evening dance, she shook her head and waved them away.

Charlie cursed under his breath. He had not wanted to come into the heather and yet he had. He had not wanted to do good and yet good had been done. He resolved to fight the heather's power. He would ply Patrick with drink, persuade Tom the Blacksmith's son that Mary Feltham was in love with him. He would piss down the well and smash the windows of the church. He went to stand, but someone was walking past, so he ducked back down. It was Patrick.

"Burn the heather," Charlie whispered.

But that wasn't me, he thought. I don't want him to burn the heather. He tried to say these thoughts aloud, but all he could manage was; "Burn the heather, Patrick. Burn the heather now."

But that is not my voice, he thought.

"Burn it now Patrick."

It was never my voice.

"Burn it all."

It was the voice of the heather.

"Burn it."

It is not me. I am not speaking.

"Burn it."

And yet it is my voice.

"Burn the heather."

It is my voice.

"Burn."

I am the voice of the heather.

Patrick struck a match and threw it into the heather. It crackled and blazed into life, spreading across fields and hills. Smoke rose into the air, danced around the heads and into the nostrils and ears of the villagers. Later they swore that they could hear, coming out of the smoke, the whispered scream of a child repeating over and over;

"This is not my voice."

No one saw Charlie Ellerton ever again.

But they heard him.

They heard him when they put a sprig of heather next to their smoke-kissed ears.

Heather and Bramble

The Blackberry Swim

The Blackberry Swim

It is said that those who bring in the blackberries at harvest time have the toughest hands. Hardened by the sun or wind, they become immune to the most vicious thorns. The skin is thick. Even a sharpened blade struggles to make a cut. A delicate city-dweller would weep after walking only several feet into bramble. Their clothes would snag, the scratches, pricking and blood-letting would become all too much for their pale-white rose-petal complexions. The blackberry harvester would amble through, as though walking through a field of daffodils.

There are a few young gentlemen who are known to strip to their undergarments and partake in the "Blackberry Swim". This involves climbing a tree amidst the bramble, and spying out the land before plunging into the densest and most unkind thorns. These young gentlemen then attempt to float on the bramble without touching the ground, rotating arms and rolling torsos over the waves of blackberry. Scratches and cuts become marks of bravery. Skin becomes toughened leather. After several years the bramble becomes nothing to their skin, a downy soft eiderdown of feather and air.

It was to a family of blackberry pickers that a young child was born. Tradition had it that a new-born had branches of bramble placed in the cot. The cries and screams would soon diminish. The little mite would grow to love the smell of the sweet fruit. The child would quickly grow accustomed to the caress of thorn against soft skin. This child was not like his six older siblings. How he cried. It was expected at first of course, but he never stopped. The father suggested taking the bramble from around the pillow to ease his pain, but the mother, a stickler for tradition, insisted on putting in more twisted branches. The child wailed. The mother wrapped bramble around her calloused hands so even when she picked him from the cradle he could not escape the terrible cut of the unforgiving blackberry.

You may think the mother cruel. But this was what *her* mother had done and her mother before her. So she changed the bloodied sheets every day, knowing that gradually the child's cries would diminish. The bramble would be as a soft blanket to her sweet child. A comfort. A balm.

But the cries of the child did not quieten. Every day the sheets were spattered with blood. Every day the mother would put fresh bramble in the cot. The child learnt to lay completely still, a slight movement could cause a scratch, a bleed, a scar. The father could bear the cries no longer. Tears pricked his eyes. He took out the bramble as soon as his wife's back was turned, so that the poor child could sleep.

Every day was the same. Mother would put in fresh bramble. Once she had left the room, Father would strip the thorns from every tangled branch before placing them back into the cradle. He persuaded his wife to let him take over the brambling of the cot. Being a busy woman, slaving over boiling pots of blackberry jam, brewing blackberry wine or mixing up batches of refreshing blackberry cordial, she was more than happy to let him take over the care of his son. She had grown distant now, the boy was not like her other sons.

They ran into the blackberry, shirts off, arms outstretched, letting the thorns caress and stroke their skin. No, if father wanted this screaming anomaly, he was welcome to it.

So father brought up his son with great care. He learnt quickly that even a little cut would gush blood and without care would not stop bleeding for days.

Mother sent her children into the bramble to pick berries from a very early age. Mother's jam and cordial were the talk of the county. Demand was high. So it was, in the child's seventh year, he was sent out to harvest.

Father knew that his son would be grievously hurt by the work, so he gave him a book with words and pictures and sat him under a tree, before bidding him farewell. Father carried two baskets. His own and his son's. At the end of the day he would give his son the fullest basket to show Mother. She was so pleased. She ruffled the boy's hair with pride and hailed him "King of the Blackberry".

But this subterfuge could not last. Several seasons passed and in his ninth year, the secret was revealed. Mother came out to give her family some freshly brewed cordial. She found the boy sitting under a tree reading a picture book about the life of Saint Paul. When he saw her approaching his eyes grew wide with terror. She asked him what he was doing. Nothing but a half-mumbled squeak escaped from his lips. Father strolled out of the meadow, two full baskets in his hands. Mother looked at her husband and then looked down at the quaking boy.

There was a long silence.

Mother put her fingers to her lips and gave a long whistle. A distant shout, a muffled curse, and the rustling of bramble branches, heralded the arrival of the six other sons. They ran to their mother's side, mouths hanging open, eager to please.

"I think it's time your lazy and cowardly brother had a swim," she said.

Father's eyes widened. He dropped the baskets to the floor. Blackberries spilled onto the grass. The six brothers cheered, lifted the boy onto their shoulders, chanting "Blackberry swim! Blackberry swim!"

Father tried to block their path but they pushed past him, knocking him to the floor. The boy could hear father's screams as he was carried into the depths of the blackberry.

The brothers were joyous. They smiled at the boy. When he looked frightened they told him not to worry. They too had been scared at the first swim. The maze of bramble led them to an ancient oak. They placed the boy on a branch above their heads and clambered up to join him. The boy shivered and sobbed, staring wildly at the masses of thorns below him. As he saw his grinning brothers approaching, he snapped out of his reverie and began to climb into the upper branches. The brothers laughed, shouting encouragement.

"That's right! It's more fun the higher you fall!"

His eldest brother took a different route and was soon far above him hollering, "Watch this!"

The brother edged out to the end of a branch, stretching out both his arms, before pitching forward, plummeting down with a yell of joy and allowing the tangled thorns to embrace him. The brothers cheered and clapped. The eldest rested on the bramble, flapping his arms up and down, laughing with glee as the prickles playfully scratched at his leathered hide.

A whoop sounded above the boy's head and another brother sailed down into the bramble. The boy could contain himself no longer. He had been holding back the tears but now let out a great howl of terror. The youngest of the six brothers crawled out on the branch next to him.

"It's all right," he said. "I was scared the first time I took the swim. It's nothing to be frightened of. It hurts at first but it hardens the skin. You need it if you're going to be a blackberry picker."

"But..." the boy sobbed. "I don't want to pick blackberries."

The whoops of the two brothers below ceased. Indeed it seemed as if the air itself was still. His brother was silent. The crickets stopped their song. The birds all closed their beaks. His brother broke the silence.

"You don't want to?"

"N-no."

"Why not?"

"It hurts. I b-bleed at the slightest scratch. Do you have any idea what bramble thorns would do to me? Look!"

The boy held out his palm for his brother to see. It was red with blood. His brother gasped.

"How did you do this?"

"A slight scratch while climbing the tree. To you, to anyone it would be nothing. To me..."

The boy watched as blood trickled from his hand to the bramble below.

His brother shook his head.

"We didn't know. I'm sorry."

He held out his hand for the boy to take. Reaching out the boy overbalanced, wobbling. His foot slipped. With a cry he fell into the bushes below. The brother screamed. The boy hit the brambles in a shower of scarlet. The thorns dug deep. He thrashed in pain. The brother dived down and landed beside him telling the boy to hold still. To keep calm.

But every attempt to move the boy from the bramble bush only resulted in more scratches. Within a matter of seconds the boy was unrecognisable, covered in his own blood, the thorns tugging and biting at his skin. Flesh was exposed. The more he struggled the deeper the thorns sawed at him, his screams rent the valley. The boy could sense his father near, see him through the red glow that was his sight. He could hear the sobs over his own gurgling moans.

"What did you do?"

"He fell father. It was an accident."

He could feel seven pairs of hands working at the bramble gently, prying it away. He could hear the curses as fresh blood spurted from new wounds. It didn't hurt anymore. He was just blood now. Skin had unravelled like a poorly knitted dishcloth. The flesh was torn and exposed the bone. Everything felt distant. He was only blood now, bubbling on the bone, dripping onto the bramble, pooling on the soil below, melting into the earth. He found the roots and seeped into every tendon, running up the stem, into the tangle, into the bramble, to every thorn, to every bud, to every wide green leaf. Swimming in the blackberry.

Father picked up the bones of his youngest son and cradled them to his chest. His sons followed him out of the bramble in solemn procession. Mother stood waiting by the tree. When she saw the body of her son she shook her head, turned and walked back into the house to attend to her simmering pots of jam.

Father buried the boy under the tree where he had read his books. Mother was silent for two days. On the third day she ordered her sons back out into the meadow, expressing concern that they would miss the harvest.

The berries around the ancient oak were a dark, purplish red. They were richer and darker than any of the other berries in the bramble. The bramble was abundant with them. The boys shivered with fear, remembering what had happened here. They didn't dare touch them and so called their mother to look. Strolling over to the spot where the boy had burst, she glanced at the berries before popping one in her mouth. A groan of pleasure escaped from her lips, her eyes rolled back in her head, eyelids flickered heavily.

"I have never tasted the like," she marvelled.

She took more and more, stuffing them into her maw, one after another.

"Baskets," she managed through overflowing lips. "Fill the baskets."

The boys edged forward. They began to clear the bramble of berries. They did not dare taste them but filled basket after basket. The harvest seemed infinite. Once emptied into the kitchen pots more would be filled. The blackberries multiplied. The brothers picked constantly for three days without rest.

In the kitchen, Mother heated the stove and prepared the blackberries for cooking. She discovered that she did not need to sieve away the seeds as there were none in any of the berries picked. She needed to add no sugar as they were sweet enough.

As she made jam, she constantly ate. As she poured berries into the pot, she would pop another into her mouth. As she stirred the sticky broth, she would work her way through another bowlful. As she decanted the jam into jars, she chewed and sucked her way through the harvest.

Father entered the kitchen that night to find her surrounded by jars of bright scarlet blackberry jam. Mother had a pot open and was scooping still cooling jam with her finger and licking it off. Every time she gave a moan of pleasure. Father opened a jar and had a sniff.

"Think these'll sell well?" he asked.

"Sell?" said Mother, jam smeared around her mouth. "Sell? These won't be sold my love. Oh no, they're too good to sell."

Father dipped his finger into the jam and pulled it out with a satisfying squelch. He looked at the scarlet jelly congealing on his fingers.

"Put that back." Mother's voice was cold.

"Just want to see what all the fuss is about, dear," said Father taking a hearty lick.

Pain flared across Father's head. Pain and a terrible distorted ringing in his ears. He found himself on the hard tiled floor. Looking up he saw his wife glaring down at him, the large pan she had struck him with, held tightly in her hand.

"Put it back," she snarled. "Every drop. Every smidgeon. Every taste."

Father staggered to his feet, cursing under his breath and wiped his finger on the edge of the jar. Mother snatched it away, swiftly replacing the lid. She went back to her own jar, pulled out a spoon and tucked in. Father shook his aching head, left the room and stumbled up to bed.

The brothers woke up early the next morning and rushed down for breakfast before they began harvesting again. The kitchen was a mess. Empty jam-jars were strewn across the floor. They looked around for Mother and were able to locate her by following the sound of gentle and contented snoring coming from the floor by the stove. Lying on the tiles, a beatific smile on her jam-sodden lips, was Mother, hands resting on her distended stomach, tiny burps and grunts emanating from her mouth and behind. There wasn't a single berry left from yesterday's harvest. Every jam jar was licked clean.

Shaking their heads, the boys armed themselves with baskets and walked out into the blackberry. They avoided picking berries from around the ancient oak.

Mother slept for two days. Father had found her and dragged her up to bed. She awoke refreshed and back to her old self. She ordered the brothers to pick more blackberries and set about cleaning the jam jars and pots. Mother made up new batches of blackberry jam and cordial using her traditional recipe. She did not mention her gluttony or the long sleep it had put her in. No-one else dared to broach the subject.

It was while she was chopping onions for her county-famous onion and blackberry chutney that the unheard of occurred. The knife she was using scraped against her finger. She barely noticed it at first. A simple scratch from a knife normally meant nothing, but after a couple of moments it became clear that things were different as the chopped onions became spattered in red. She looked at her leathery finger in confusion. Blood gushed from the little cut. She sucked the blood from the end of her finger to stem the flow but it poured into her mouth. She pressed it hard which seemed to have some effect, though she could feel it throbbing underneath the pressure. When she released her hold a shower of blood spurted into her surprised face.

Mother ran up to the boy's bedroom and looked through his drawers. Father had secreted bandages in here, she knew it. She gave a little cry of joy when she saw a roll of bandages behind some thick woollen socks. She pulled it out and began wrapping it around her finger, noting with some distaste the puddles of blood on the floorboards.

Finally the bleeding stopped. The bandage was seeped in blood but there was no more dripping. Mother fastened the bandage by tucking it inside itself, rather than using a pin. She grew steadily nervous at the thought of anything sharp.

Mother made up a jug of cordial and took it out to her sons. She approached the blackberry field with some trepidation. After pausing for a moment, she shrugged off her fear as nonsensical and strolled calmly into the bramble. She didn't notice the first few scratches but her sons looked shocked to see her face, arms and legs dripping in scarlet and glistening in the midday sun.

"What have you done?" they cried.

She looked down at herself and gasped. The jug of cordial fell to the floor.

"What is happening?" she murmured before collapsing in a dead faint.

The brothers carried her to bed, wrapping her afflicted legs tight in bandages. The bleeding seemed to stop, though all the bandages were clearly soaked in blood.

When Father got home the brothers took him upstairs. Mother was shivering and sobbing on the bed. Father looked on her with pity. He tended her day and night, gently cleaning the blood from her face and offering her cordial until her strength returned.

She awoke one night in a fever. The itching under her bandages was driving her into a frenzy. She stumbled down the stairs, moaning and cursing. If she could just get at the cause of her discomfort. Mother slumped into her favourite chair in the kitchen. She untucked the bandage around her finger. When she found the final layer she discovered that the congealed blood had fused it to her skin. She picked at it until she could find an edge and peeled it away. Underneath there seemed to be more bloody congealed bandage, so she pulled

97

and unwound it further. The itch was still intense. A thick strip of skin pulled away in her fingers, but still the itching grew. So she continued to tug until the flesh and skin unwrapped, revealing the stark white of her bone beneath.

Mother was in a daze. She blinked at the bone. She felt no pain and the terrible itching in the tip of her finger had stopped. The sensation in her legs, arms and face was unbearable. She scratched at her legs but felt no relief. She began to unravel the dry bandages frantically. She tugged at cloth to get to the skin. She picked at the skin to get to the flesh. She tore at flesh to get to the bone. Blood pooled around her feet. The white of her bones stood in sharp contrast against the dark of her flesh and the deep scarlet of her blood. The itching in her legs ceased. There was no pain. Only relief.

But her face. Oh her face. How it itched. How it crawled with tiny spider feet. She scratched at the bandages on her cheeks, forehead and nose, pulling them away in a frenzy. Tugging and tearing. Pinching and pulling. Scratching, picking, shredding. Over and over, faster and faster until she had finished. The itching stopped. She sat quite still, relaxed at last, a grinning bloodied skull atop of a scarlet spattered nightdress.

Heather and Bramble

The Heart of the Blackberry Field

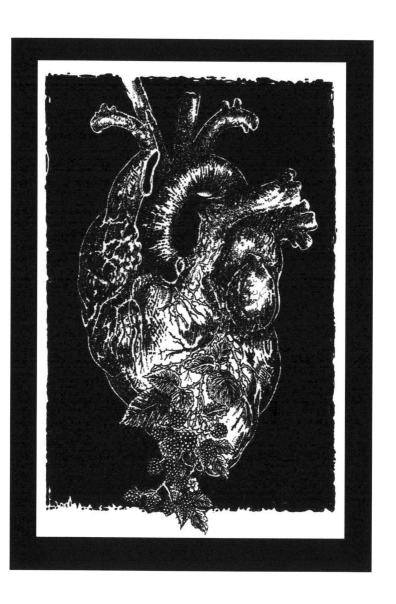

The Heart of the Blackberry Field

Peter Ostler had moved to the village from the south of the country. He was given a warm welcome from the villagers, but he did not fully understand their ways nor they his. He had left his birthplace in Hastings (which he had abandoned at fourteen years of age following an altercation with a costermonger; the consequences of which resulted in a permanent and livid scar that ran from the centre of his left cheek to his chin) and wandered country lanes for several years until he finally settled in the village in the centre of the Black Meadow.

He had become adept at many jobs on his travels. At fifteen he had worked as an apprentice to the Blacksmith in Bishop's Storford for over a year, learning aspects of the craft that would prove useful to him when he moved on. The strange and affectionate attentions of the Blacksmith's young and beautiful wife caused the lad much consternation and resulted in him making a swift exit from his master's employ. This led him to run further north. He settled in Ely for about six months cleaning out the pigs for a farmer, a profession, it was remarked, worthy of his family name. It was the cloying smell that clung to his clothes, coated the insides of his nostrils and flavoured his food and drink with a constant tinge of excrement, that caused him to wander further afield. He thought he would settle in Sleaford and stayed there for two and a half years working as a groom for a local baron. But when the kindly chief groom was replaced by a foul-mouthed ex-serviceman, who taught with the whip rather than the tongue, he knew that it was time to move on. It was several months of travelling, working and occasional begging that led him to the North York Moors and finally to the embrace of the village in the centre of the Black Meadow.

The village was surrounded on all sides by swathes of blackberry. When he enquired in the local tavern about work, the villagers grinned broadly, poured him a goblet of blackberry wine and patted his back, telling him he had come just at the right time. The harvest was excellent this year and so the picking, the harvesting, the pressing, the preserving and the brewing would prove to be a mammoth task. One that would require many hands and a hard worker would be welcome. So it was that Pater Ostler settled in the village in the heart of the Black Meadow. He was given a room in the farmer's house just above the stables. He soon became used to the rhythms of the village. He helped with the harvest, with the cooking, with the bottling and with the trips to market. When the bramble was growing he maintained the well-trodden paths between the tangled rows. He joined in the singing in warm Octobers, he sang out for the dead at Yuletide, he left out the carved pumpkins for the Coyle. He did all of these things and felt happy and content.

It was in the third year, in the village, that his eye fell upon Ruth Thorpe, the daughter of the local grocer. He had noticed her before, indeed they had made several journeys into Whitby and Robin Hood's Bay together, armed with jars, bottles, tarts and pies for selling in the local markets. He had thought her pretty, but his mind had been focussed on making his way in this village. But now that he was settled and felt part of this community and even part of the farmer's family, he began to relax, he began to notice. He lifted his head and looked around. He saw the beauty of the tangle of bramble, the desolate and romantic ache of the heather beyond. He saw her, her dark brown, almost black hair, green eyes and pale petal soft skin. He saw her smile when she looked at him and he sent his own smile back to her.

On the journey on the cart to Whitby, he felt her hand upon his arm as he urged the pony forward. He felt her head upon his shoulder as they made their tired journey back. He felt her warm lips against his cheek before she turned to go into her house. Their conversations grew beyond shy mumbles and he began to learn more about her. He discovered that she loved the rain, good heavy rain, not a drizzle. She feared the mist, though she enjoyed its mystery. She was sick to the back teeth of blackberries and longed for apple chutney. She had a sweet tooth and looked forward to their journeys to Whitby where he would buy a basket of cinder toffee and a bottle of sweet apple sherry. The village whispered about coming nuptials and the courtship was indeed moving towards that point but something happened that caused a momentous pause. The farmer, an elderly gentleman, passed away on a spring morning, his middle-aged son took on the workings of the whole farm, meaning that Peter Ostler was given the task of maintaining the blackberry himself. This was a huge responsibility for one man as the village's prosperity relied upon the flow of blackberry. Peter Ostler had managed many of the pathways under the farmer's tutelage, but now he would be in charge of the field and its stock. He took the new job very seriously and asked the farmer to sit down with him and give clear instructions as to how he would continue to build on the earlier successes.

The farmer was very pleased to share his knowledge and gladly laid out the rules and structures for maintaining the blackberry. The width of the paths, the maintenance of the pruning shears, the optimum picking times and the upkeep of the baskets were now all in Peter Ostler's hands. But, there was one vital thing that Peter Ostler should be aware of. When in the centre of the field he should utterly ignore anything he might hear.

So Peter Ostler worked hard over the following months settling into his new routine. After some time he was able to begin courting Ruth Thorpe anew. She understood his absence when he took over from the farmer and indeed saw it as the mark of a serious and committed man. So it was, in the fourth year since he had arrived on the Black Meadow, that Peter Ostler and Ruth Thorpe were married. Never was there a prouder bearer of that pungent surname than Peter's darling Ruth. The farmer gave him and his wife a sweet cottage on the edge of his land. Everything was wonderful.

It was on his inspection of the growing bramble that Peter Ostler first noticed the noise. He found himself in the centre of the blackberry field and could hear a dull throbbing sound. He remembered the words of his employer and put it out of his mind. However, over the coming weeks he dwelt on the sound, pondering on it over his morning porridge, thinking about it as he walked the rows, listening to the dull repetitive throb in his memory, as he lay next to his beautiful wife at night time. It pulled and pulled at him. So it was that he found himself again in the centre of the blackberry field. He stood still, cocked his head to one side, listening intently. There it was, the throb, throb, throb. A heartbeat. Peter Ostler placed his hand against his own heart, perhaps in the stillness it was his own pulse that he heard. But the throb of his heart was not in time with the strange external beat.

When he returned to the farmhouse, the farmer grabbed his arm. "I saw you," he said.

Peter Ostler expressed his confusion.

The farmer looked angry. "I saw you in the centre of the field. Standing still. Listening. You were listening, weren't you?"

Peter Ostler nodded slowly. "I heard..." he began.

"I don't want to know what you heard. You heard nothing, do you understand? Nothing!"

But Peter didn't understand, even when the farmer threatened him with expulsion from his service he was still filled with curiosity. The farmer told him to keep his mind on his occupation, he knew he was a good man but in this he must follow his lead. Peter promised that he would never stand and listen in the centre of the blackberry field again. The farmer made him swear and Peter Ostler swore.

But something had happened to Peter. All the while that the farmer was speaking, he could hear, ever so faintly, the beat of a heart that was not his own. And, as he lay down that night, he could hear the pulse again. He pressed his ear against his wife's bosom, listening to her sweet blood pumping through that most miraculous organ. But underneath it, there it was, that dull

thud, thud,
thud, thud,
thud, thud,
thud, thud.

Slower than his wife's and more distinct than his own. He closed his eyes and tried to think of other things, but the beating increased in volume. So loud now, so intense. He folded his pillow around his head, holding the edges tight against his ears but to no avail. The pulse increased further. He leapt from the bed, blindly ignoring the cry of alarm from his wife or her calming hand upon his arm. He ran from the cottage. The noise was deafening. So loud, so relentless. He clamped his hands over his ears. Running panicked into the field, where was the source of this horrible sound? Where was the source of this beating heart? He ran towards the centre of the field and, with every step, the beat became louder and louder. So loud that he feared that his head would split apart from the relentless pressure of the

thud, thud,
thud, thud,
thud, thud,
thud, thud.

He stood panting. Screaming at the sky, trying to drown out the sound. He searched around frantically, desperate to find the source of the beat.

His ear was drawn to a patch of bramble close by. The bramble was ancient and thick – as thick as the trunk of an old birch. He put his head to the ground and, sure enough, it was near-deafening here, but not the source. He pulled at the brambles near him, revealing another thick, old bramble trunk. Moving around he found another, and another until he stood, hands scratched and bloody, gazing upon a circle of seven bramble trunks, each perfectly placed and equidistant from each other with a six foot wide circle in their centre. A circle devoid of bramble. He squeezed through the tight gap between the bramble trunks and found himself within the circle. The beating was unbearable now. He could feel the pulse beneath his feet. Crouching down he could see, by the grey light of the moon, the soil was rising and falling in time with the beat of this extraordinary pulse. Peter Ostler could bear it no longer. Ignoring the pain in his thorn-scratched hands he tore at the earth, tearing up clods of soil in fury and terror. He dug down a good few feet until he found his excavation halted by thick bramble roots converging on a central point. He cleared away the remaining mud, revealing the cause of his misery at last. Leaping back in shock he became entangled with the tendrils emerging from the thick bramble trunks behind him. Taking a gulp of air he braved himself to look again. There in the hole, with seven bramble roots running through it like veins, was a single beating heart.

This was the cause of his pain, this abomination, this travesty of nature. Peter Ostler resolved himself. He reached down into the hole and gripped the beating and surprisingly warm heart in his hand

and pulled. The heartbeat quickened. The leaves on the bramble shivered and shook. Tendrils of bramble waved, scratching against his face. Still he pulled. Over and over. Harder and harder. Until, with a wrench and a sickening tear it came free. He fell upon his back, panting furiously. The heartbeat suddenly ceased.

Peter Ostler flung the heart from him and wiped his bloodied hands on his nightshirt. He washed his hands in the trough outside the house before returning to his wife, placating her with soft apologies and sinking into a deep sleep.

There was some consternation on the farm the next day. His wife had shaken him awake in some worry. There was a problem with the blackberry field, she told him. Something was very wrong. Running out into the mid-morning sun he saw what she was referring to. The blackberry field was a sickly yellow – all the leaves were on the turn. The farmer and all the labourers were out on the edge looking over the field, muttering darkly.

"It's only May," one of them said.

"Aye, and there were nowt wrong yestereve," grumbled another.

Peter Ostler walked towards the farmer who squinted at him in the mid-morning sun. "Where've you been?"

"I just awoke."

"Not like you, Peter. You unwell?"

"My night was unsettled, sir. I am sorry."

"It surely was unsettled, Peter, look at this."

Peter followed the sweep of his hand. The entire meadow had changed from green to yellow overnight.

"What could do this?"

The farmer gazed over the wilting blackberry, "Never seen the like of this before. Heard about it though. My father saw this the once."

"What is it? A blight? Are they missing something? Water? Compost?"

"There's very little stops a bramble, very little. One will grow and keep growing for years and years, they will stretch and find root wherever they can in driest earth to dampest mud, to deepest shade or harshest sun. They prevail. But within the space of a week all of this will be dry and dead. There will be no more blackberry on the meadow."

"There must be something we can do."
The farmer looked at Peter. He took a step closer to him.

"Ruth tells me you were out of bed in the night."

"I was, but…"

"You heard it didn't you. You heard the beating heart of the blackberry field."

"You know?"

"It got too loud for you, son didn't it? It happens – and when it does… well it's time for a change."

"A change?"

"A change of heart."

Peter gaped at the farmer. He gulped. "There was… there was an abomination in the field. Seven bramble trunks and between them a beating heart in the ground. I had to make it stop."

The farmer nodded. "It is just as my father said."
"It is?"

"Aye. When the bramble sings out then he who hears the song shall serve the field."

"I don't understand," stammered Peter.

111

"You will," said the farmer. He nodded to his labourers who stepped forward in anticipation. "It is time for the turn of the bramble," he announced. "We have waited for sixty years and the time is upon us. We will carouse tonight and tomorrow the bramble will be new and green and all will be well." He slapped Peter Ostler on the back. "We are glad you came to us Peter, for your hard work, diligence and character, your big heart. You will bring prosperity for many years to come."

Four of the labourers ran out to the barn and brought out two barrels of blackberry wine. Wives set to baking and cooking - children played on the edges of the meadow. By late afternoon instruments were playing, voices were singing, food was consumed and much drink gulped down. Peter found that his goblet was never empty. His head span. He danced with his wife and she kissed him hard and desperate, weeping copious tears. But Peter's head was muddled; he could not fathom the reason for her tears, nor could he offer comfort to her. Eventually, full of food and wine, chuckling softly to himself, he sank down upon a bench and found himself falling into a deep sleep.

Peter Ostler awoke on his back. Naked and cold. He found that his arms were stretched above his head and tied to something. His feet were also bound. He craned his neck to look about. His head throbbed. He could see that his feet were tied to the trunks of two large bramble bushes. His arms were similarly bound. He was lying on soft soil in the middle of a circle of seven thick bramble trunks. With swift realisation he saw where he was. He could feel a hole in the earth underneath his back, parallel with the position of his heart. He screamed out for help.

There was a rustle of leaves next to him and the farmer poked his head between the branches. He held in his hand a watering can which he used to water the soil around the prone form of Peter Ostler. Peter asked him for help, asked to be untied, but the farmer just smiled, continuing to walk around the perimeter of the circle, humming a merry tune and watering as he walked.

Peter wept.

Several hours passed. He felt a hand grasp his. Leaning his head back he could see Ruth's tearful face smiling at him as she stretched her arm between two of the vast old bramble trunks. She told him she loved him. He begged to be untied. She shook her head and walked away, weeping softly.

At the dawn of the next day Peter Ostler awoke from a fitful sleep. He could feel something pressing into the small of his back. Something sharp and pointed pushing, ever so slightly, against his bare skin. As the day progressed so the pressure became more intense until, in the late afternoon, it became a pain, at first soft and throbbing but later hard and unrelenting. It was at dusk that he felt his skin break and tear. He cried out. A raw animal scream. The sensation was so extreme that he drifted into blackness, waking only once the pain began to numb. Now he felt pressure from two other points close to the first. As the night drew on the skin tore again and again. Four more points pressed against the skin of his back. It would be only a matter of time before they too broke through.

He could feel them pushing through his flesh as the days passed. Strangely the pain began to dissipate and he did not feel hungry or thirsty. He began to notice that the leaves on the bramble were growing greener. He was no longer able to move his head. He could feel the bramble roots pushing further and further inside. They had all found the heart now but they continued to shift around his body slowly.

It was on the tenth day when they punctured his lungs that Peter Ostler finally expired. His brain was a mass of tangled root by now so he was completely unaware of this development. The brambles had grown through and over him, poking through the sockets of his eyes, snaking into his ears and out through his nose and mouth. But through all of this trauma his heart never stopped beating. It never stopped. It still beats now. And the bramble is green, the blackberry healthy and Peter Ostler is settled; a fruitful and loyal heart of the blackberry field.

The Mysteries of Fylingdales House

He Took Her Hand

He took her hand

A lady fair, she'd travell'd far, she'd travell'd long
and hard.
She had the name and the address writ roughly on
a card.
She look'd in horror at the house and trembl'd in
her fear,
So tall, so dark, so steep'd in doom, so much
devoid of cheer.
She rapp'd upon the old oak door and listen'd for a
sound,
A little cough, a useless foot a'dragging at the
ground.
The door creak'd open, eyes peered out beneath a
wrinkl'd brow.
A gentleman, old and bent he gave a creaking bow.
The lady fair, she stumbl'd back and turn'd at once
to run.
The gentleman, he shook his head and stepp'd into
the sun.

He took her hand.
He took her hand.
He roughly took her hand.
He pull'd her deep into the house
And roughly took her hand.

The lady fair, she sat so still with tears staining her
face.
The gentleman, he tried to smile, but a smile was
out of place.
And both of them, they sat quite mute and nary
made a sound.
He sat and studied her sweet face while she
studied the ground.
He gestured at the treasures that adorn'd the walls
about,
He pointed at them, then to her, ensuring that no
doubt
Would be at all within her mind that all of this was
theirs,
And when tomorrow's work was done he'd guide
her up the stairs.
And they would share a sweet embrace that all
good wives must take,
But as these words escap'd his mouth, her hands
began to shake.

He squeez'd her hand.
He squeez'd her hand.
He firmly squeez'd her hand.
"To calm her nerves" he told himself,
He squeez'd her shaking hand.

The priest inton'd his fateful words before the tiny
crowd.
The old man's sister wip'd her eyes and blew her
nose too loud.
He spoke his vows in noble tones, so clear and true
and bright.
She mumbl'd hers in sobs of shame, of fear at her
sad plight.
The ring it scratch'd against her skin and fitted
poorly there,
And as he tugg'd the veil away it pull'd hard at her
hair.
He tried to kiss her on the mouth, she turn'd her
head away,
He tried to kiss her on the cheek, (for far too long
they say).
They turn'd to face the tiny crowd and shuffle
down the aisle,
He grinn'd with pride at his sweet prize. She
couldn't even smile.

He held her hand.
He held her hand.
He proudly held her hand.
He dragg'd her slowly from the church
And proudly held her hand.

The days they turn'd fast into months, those
months turn'd into years.
The time she spent lock'd in her room was
measur'd out in tears.
Ev'ry night his wrinkl'd fist would rap upon the
door,
He'd moan and whine that she was his, that she
was his by law.
But she was steadfast, she was cruel, for this was
not her choice,
For no-one once, not even once, had listen'd to her
voice.
He walk'd and pac'd, so tense and raging, at her
chilling mood.
He knock'd and kick'd her door so hard, he begg'd
to please intrude.
At supper once, her silent frown caus'd him to
curse and swear,
He swept the dishes from their place and pull'd her
from her chair.

He hurt her hand.
He hurt her hand.
He, careless, hurt her hand.
He cast her hard upon the floor
And hurt her lovely hand.

He let her be for some time then, did not disturb
                                        her door,
He did not moan that she was his, that she was his
                                        by law.
And in the day she walk'd about the garden and
                                        the field,
Away from the oppressive house wherein her fate
                                        was seal'd.
He watch'd her from the window as she trod her
                                        maudlin way,
She felt his eyes upon her form throughout the
                                        lonely day.
One morn she ventur'd further still beyond his
                                        longing gaze,
And came upon a broken stile before a misty haze.
Before the fog, a silhouette was standing on the
                                        grass,
A swarthy man, so tall and fair, he would not let
                                        her pass.

He rais'd his hand.
He rais'd his hand.
He firmly rais'd his hand.
"You must not venture further dear"
He said and rais'd his hand.

The stranger stepp'd much closer still and pointed
                                    at the mist,
He shook his head and talk'd her through a
                                    terrifying list
Of creatures dark and fates so foul that lurk'd
                                    within the cloud,
Of houses and a village green within the parlous
                                    shroud.
The lady fair, with eyes so wide, relish'd each tale
                                    unfold,
She watch'd the tall man's face and hands unwrap
                                    these tales untold.
And when at last, his warning spent, he turn'd to
                                    walk away,
She took a step, her hand reach'd out, she begg'd
                                    him please to stay.
She told him of the sour old man, of the house
                                    upon the hill.
She told him of the lonely nights, the unrelenting
                                    chill.

She took his hand.
She took his hand.
She, desperate, took his hand.
She pull'd him close and kiss'd him hard
And, desperate, took his hand.

The old man's eyes burn'd into hers as she stepp'd
through the door.
She smil'd to cover up her guilt and gaz'd hard at
the floor.
He pointed to the trees beyond the grounds, he
pointed where
Her love and she had kiss'd so sweet, so free
without a care.
He growl'd at her, he bore his teeth, he swore
under his breath,
He told her that one dalliance more would mean
her certain death.
She gasp'd at this and star'd in shock and wonder
at his mind.
She ask'd the old man why he thought she could
be so unkind.
He snarl'd again and shook his head. He pull'd her
up the stair,
Up and up a winding route to his dark and lonely
lair.

He rais'd his hand.
He rais'd his hand.
He, anger'd, rais'd his hand.
He pointed to the telescope,
Then struck her with his hand.

She stagger'd from the shock and swore a curse
upon her foe,
She stumbl'd fast across the room to avoid the
coming blow.
She grabb'd the 'scope from off its stand and rais'd
it in the air.
The old man cried "For the sake of God, please you
must take care!"
She laugh'd at him and spat deep scarlet from
between her teeth.
She brought the 'scope a'crashing down upon his
head beneath.
The lenses shatter'd, his head it split, a jagged
wound appear'd.
She struck him hard again, again, until her heart
was cheer'd.
And when at last her work was done, she look'd at
the dead man,
She shudder'd at her fate because this had not
been her plan.

She wash'd her hands.
She wash'd her hands.
She carefully wash'd her hands.
She wip'd all trace of blood away
And carefully wash'd her hands.

She hurried to her chamber fast to take what she
                                            would need.
She ran downstairs and out the door with
                                    unrelenting speed.
She scurried to the trees beyond to find the fog-
                                        bound field,
To find the man whose expert kiss her broken
                                    heart had heal'd.
She waited by the tree and look'd beyond the
                                        broken stile,
The wind it blew, the mist it rose, she waited a long
                                            while.
She thought she heard a sound within the cold
                            and dark'ning mist,
The sweet sound of children laughing, a shout, a
                                    lover's tryst.
She stepp'd towards the broken stile to take a
                                    closer look,
And then she stopp'd and heard a voice behind
                                her. How it shook!

He took her hand.
He took her hand.
He gently took her hand.
He begg'd her not to leave his side,
And gently held her hand.

127

Her lover spoke in hush'd dark tones of the village
in the haze,
Of how it came in clouds of mist and stay'd out
there for days.
And then at once this mist would go and with it
went that place.
She smil'd at that and told him of her crime, of her
disgrace,
That all she touch'd would turn to death and he
must let her go.
He shook his head, he held her hand, his tears
began to flow.
She broke away and ran from him into the meadow
black.
He follow'd fast towards the mist and tried to pull
her back.
Her hand in his, but the rest in fog, trying to move
on.
A cry of pain, a sudden hush, the dev'lish fog was
gone.

He took her hand.
He took her hand.
He held her cooling hand.
Scarlet flow'd upon the grass.
From her neatly sever'd hand.

The gentleman fell to his knees and howl'd and
                                    wept and cried.
He look'd across the empty field where the fog had
                                    lain inside.
He call'd out for the injur'd girl. He call'd and call'd
                                    again.
He shouted and he scream'd her name, but it was
                                    all in vain.
A shout came out from far behind. He would not
                                    turn to see
A group of men, with hounds and guns, were stood
                                    just by the tree,
Pointing out into the field at the man there weeping
                                    soft.
They ran towards him, flintlocks cock'd and barrels
                                    held aloft.
He turn'd his head, said not a thing a'kneeling in
                                    the mud.
They gaz'd upon the wretched man, all soaking in
                                    fresh blood.

He clutch'd her hand.
He clutch'd her hand.
He sobbing, clutch'd her hand.
They gaz'd upon this wretched man
A'clutching at her hand.

This poem is attributed to the tale of Thomas Holdsey – a commoner who was hung in 1784 in York for the murders of Lord Drysdale and his young wife Elizabeth of Fylingdales House.

This is a popular ballad that captured some of what were considered to be the incoherent ramblings of Thomas Holdsey who protested his innocence to the very end.

Interestingly, the legend also states that his corpse was buried with the severed hand of Elizabeth Drysdale, that they had never been able to pry from his hand, even after his execution. He said he was determined to return it to her.

(Taken from the notes of Roger Mullins. N.B. He transcribed this from a reading at a local tavern in Whitby in 1965)

The Mysteries of Fylingdales House

A Dead Man on the Moor

A Dead Man on the Moor

Lady Charlotte gazed from the bay window of Fylingdales Hall one cold September morning. She marvelled at the cold fog sitting low against the ground. Tufts of heather and twists of bramble poked their heads above the white. The wisps of freezing cloud swirled around a lone figure in the centre of the lower field.

It was a few hours after dawn and Lady Charlotte was already fully dressed and breakfasted. She glanced at the clock behind her, she had been staring at the unmoving form for several minutes now.

Lady Charlotte stared hard at the figure. It appeared to be a man. In the dim light of dawn it was hard to make out any features. He was definitely wearing breeches. She doubted even the Harbord girls would be so immoral as to go out in such a costume. From this distance she could see that his hair was black and unkempt. Parts of it were sticking up. She wondered for a moment whether he might be a scarecrow. Resolved, she walked over to the door and pulled the cord hanging beside it. A bell sounded in the kitchen.

A crash of a door, followed by hurried but rhythmic footsteps, announced the arrival of the Butler. He stood in the doorway.

"Ma'am?"

"Do you know where Lord Stephen's telescope is?"

"He had two Ma'am. One for the stars. I believe that is in the attic room. It is too heavy for one man to move."

"I forgot about that. He hadn't used it for so long. The climb up the stairs became too much for him."

The Butler nodded solemnly. "The other he used for navigation, Ma'am."

"That is the one I require."

"Very good Ma'am. It is with his sailing effects."

"Hurry, Stiles."

The Butler turned and sped from the room.

A moment passed. Lady Charlotte continued to look at the stranger outside. Mist sat at his feet and he appeared silhouetted before a bank of low white cloud in the distance. A footfall punctuated her thoughtful watch.

The maid was at the door. "Was there something you wanted, Ma'am?"

Lady Charlotte gestured for the maid to come to the window. She pointed at the figure in the field. "What do you make of that, Jenny?"

The Maid looked for a moment. "I do not know the man, Ma'am."

Lady Charlotte spoke quietly. "I have been watching him solidly for many minutes now and I have not yet seen him move."

"He must be very cold, Ma'am."

"You are right Jenny."

A cough at the door caused them both to turn.

"Master's telescope," the Butler intoned.

"Bring it to me Stiles."

The Butler moved over to the window. "Ma'am, there appears to be a gentleman on the lower field."

"That's right."

"Would you like me to have him removed?"

"Not yet."

Lady Charlotte held out her hand for the telescope. The Butler passed it to her and stood back with the maid while Lady Charlotte examined the man outside.

The image was blurred. An adjustment of the lenses brought a blade of grass and a wisp of mist into focus. Panning along the ground, a rush of heather and bramble through the black framed circle ended at a pair of legs. A fine set of breeches. Smart black trousers with a sharp crease at the front, little spats of mud peppering the material with flecks of brown. The black framed circle moved up to the ends of a topcoat. Crisp and black, fastened with ebony buttons all the way to the neck with a hint of elegant white shirt at the collar. A smooth grey neck. A hint of stubble on the chin. Thin lips closed tight. A shapely and impressive nose. Enormous black pupils encased in cold blue, framed in a sea of red veins. Those eyes looked directly down the lens, unblinking.

Lady Charlotte drew back from the telescope for a moment and shuddered. She put a hand to her brow. The Maid stepped forward but was waved away. Lady Charlotte returned to the task in hand.

She found that pallid grey face again. Untidy jet black hair. Grass and sprigs of heather entwined in his locks like a misshapen crown.

Lady Charlotte pulled the telescope from her eye. She handed it to the maid. "What do you make of that, Jenny?"

The maid stared at the figure for a few moments and shook her head. "He looks unwell, Ma'am."

Stiles took the telescope and perused the man closely.

"Do you know him Stiles?"

"I do not, Ma'am but I concur with Jenny. He does look most unwell. Would you like him removed?"

Lady Charlotte shook her head. "Certainly not. Clearly something ails the man." She turned to the maid. "Jenny prepare a hot bath. Stiles, I want you to bring the man inside."

"Ma'am?"

"At once."

Stiles could tell from the stern look in Lady Charlotte's eyes that she would not be moved. He nodded and sped from the room. The maid waited to be dismissed.

"Jenny, while the water is heating, ensure that a fire is lit in Lord Stephen's chamber. Find out some towels and nightwear."

"Yes, Madam."

Lady Charlotte returned her gaze to the window. She could hear the water running upstairs and the front door creaking open. She watched as Stiles - clad in longcoat, scarf, gloves and hat – walked towards the man.

Stiles was worried. He did not feel that Lady Charlotte was making a wise decision by bringing this man into the house. If he could persuade the gentleman to be on his way, then the argument would be moot. As he drew closer he was disconcerted to see that the man did not turn or even flinch at his approach. Instead he continued to stand still and stare at the house. With a growing bank of white fog behind him, the figure appeared as a shadow in sharp relief. A distant sound was carrying through the morning air, cries and crashes and far-off thunderclaps. The butler bit back his unease and hailed the stranger.

"Sir! Ahoy there! Sir!"

There was no acknowledgement from the figure.

"Sir," Stiles persisted. "What is your business here?"

The gentleman did not respond.

Stiles took a tentative step closer. "My lady has invited you into the house. You have been out here for some time and you look most unwell."

There was no sound or movement from the man.

Stiles drew nearer. He was now only two feet from the stranger. "I have come to assist you."

He reached out for the stranger's hand and was surprised at the lack of response. Stiles walked around and stood directly in front of him, blocking the figure's view of the house. He thought this might help to break the strange trance. The eyes did not flicker or blink. The head did not move. Stiles took another step forward. He was beginning to realise that the gentleman could be very unwell indeed. The butler leaned forward, scrutinising the unmoving face.

"Sir?"

There was still no response. Stiles stood there for a moment and noted two things. Firstly, the lack of breath in the air and secondly, the dry musty smell. Stiles shook his head. The unspeakable truth dawned. So surprising was this realisation that the butler found himself voicing his thoughts aloud (an affliction he normally ascribed to lunatics or worse, aesthetes).

"The poor fellow's dead."

He reached out his hand to the stranger's face and found it dry and cold to the touch. Stiles circled the figure and it was when he was studying the fellow's back that he made a horrendous discovery. A strong iron stake as tall as the corpse itself was driven deep into the ground. The pole supported the dead man. It ran up the stranger's back, underneath his topcoat and poked out of the collar. Stiles shook his head. This gentleman had been put there, placed there by some ghoulish villain. He would send for the local constable at once. As he was turning towards the house he noticed something in the corpse's breast pocket. What could have passed as a handkerchief from a distance, was in fact the corner of a small white envelope. Stiles pulled it from the pocket. He was surprised to see writing on the envelope and his surprise turned to astonishment as he saw to whom it was addressed. He ran to the house.

Lady Charlotte was standing in the entrance hall waiting.

"Well Stiles, why is the gentleman not with you?"

"The gentleman is deceased Ma'am. I am going to send for the constable at once. I will not tell you more, for it is most disturbing."

"Deceased Stiles?"

"Please Ma'am, I must send for the constable."

"What is that in your hand?"

"It is something I found on the poor fellow's person. I thought the constable should see it."

"Show it to me."

The butler hesitated. Lady Charlotte held out her hand patiently until Stiles, very reluctantly, handed it over.

Lady Charlotte blanched at the sight of her name on the envelope. She staggered slightly. Stiles rushed forward to steady her. She tore the paper and pulled out a small card from inside. She stared wildly at the message.

"The bath is ready ma'am."

The maid was standing at the bottom of the stairs.

"He won't be needing it, Jenny," Stiles said, keeping his eyes fixed on Lady Charlotte and her reaction. "Ma'am?"

Lady Charlotte held out the card for her butler to take. She gripped the edge of it very loosely between the tips of her fingers, eager for it to drop to the floor. Stiles took it gently and Jenny ran to his side.

"'Stay in the circle'," read Jenny aloud. "What does that mean?"

Lady Charlotte stumbled from the entrance hall. They followed her into the drawing room and watched as she sank onto the chaise longue.

"It means we are protected, Jenny."

The butler and the maid looked at each other without comprehension. Lady Charlotte waved at the window.

"The mist is coming. Lord Stephen told me that he had made arrangements. The mist is coming. Stay in the circle."

"There is always mist Ma'am," Stiles whispered. "This is Yorkshire after all."

"Not like this."

The butler and the maid hurried to the window. The wall of white fog behind the dead man was much closer now.

"I have never seen the like," Jenny gasped.

A low rumble could be heard outside. Stiles opened the window and gasped at the wave of sound that flooded into the house. Crashes, distant cries, crackling flames, falling rocks. Lady Charlotte put her hands to her ears. Another noise drowned out the first. A metallic scraping of iron against rock. The noise was coming from the dead man on the moor. As they watched they saw that the standing corpse was slowly rotating, turning his back on the house, turning to face the oncoming mist. The butler and the maid stood staring at the corpse as it ground to a halt.

A new and louder noise filled the air. Grinding, cracking, tearing. A small mound appeared to the left of the corpse. It began to grow. Earth fell away, revealing a shock of blonde hair. Rising further, a woman's face, unmoving, pallid, and grey. Ascending faster, until this lady - clad all in black, in the clothes she was laid out in, supported by a stake of iron – stood before them, totally lifeless, eyes unmoving in the mid-morning light. The metallic scraping continued and she slowly rotated away from the house to face the approaching fog. Another figure, a gentleman in riding habit rose to the dead man's right. As they looked on in wonder, more bodies rose. Fifty corpses supported by iron stakes, standing equidistant from each other around the perimeter of the house.

The mist continued to roll closer towards the circle of corpses. The sound from within the mist was more distinct. The grinding had ceased now. Great cries, deafening roars, crackles of electricity, explosions and laughter.

Stiles turned to Jenny. "Fetch the rifle."

Lady Charlotte shook her head. "It shall do no good."

"Madam, I have a duty to protect this house."

"We are protected."

Stiles ignored his mistress and looked at Jenny, who ran from the room.

Moments later Stiles was walking across the field towards the mist. He could just make out the shouts of Lady Charlotte, repeating over and over that he should stay in the circle. The noise coming from within the fog was ear-splitting. He poured some shot into the barrel and lifted it to his shoulder. He aimed his gun at the dead man and then, on the sound of a low guttural growl, he swung the barrel out towards the fog.

The mist was now only a few feet away from the ring of corpses. It drew closer and closer. Stiles stepped forward and looked into the face of the dead man. There was a slight twitch of muscle, a slow creak of movement and it turned its head to look at him. It blinked as though suddenly awake. The attention of the dead man fell on the mist. Its mouth suddenly dropped open. Glancing to his left, Stiles could see that the blonde corpse was doing the same, as were the rider and the many others around the outside of Fylingdales Hall. All the corpses stood with jaws open wide.

A low guttural sound escaped from the mouths of the dead. Growing louder and louder. The mist kept on coming, but it did not enter the circle of corpses, instead it swept around the outside. Stiles stood still. He dropped his gun to the ground. Looking up into the sunlit sky he could see that the house stood in a perfect circle of daylight in the midst of an impenetrable fog.

The corpses sang.

Above: A recently released photo of the Brightwater team taken in 1932. *(Source: The Brightwater Archive)*
Below: Roger Mullins taking readings on the moor in 1969. *(Photo courtesy of Philip Hull)*

Roger Mullins relaxing before venturing onto the moors. *(Photo courtesy of Derek Mullins.)*

Above: Mysterious ghostly aircraft which look very similar to this Lancaster Bomber have been seen over the North York Moors for many years. (*From the Mullins collection.*)
Below: The famous Land Spheres with unknown craft above. *(Photographer unknown.)*

The Right Honourable
Lord Thomas Brightwater
The House of Commons
LONDON

Monday 16ᵗʰ November 1931

Dear Mrs Gordon,

In response to your petition I would like to assure you that I will
undertake an investigation into the events taking place in and around
the area around Fylingdales that you refer to as "Black Meadow".

I want to re-iterate that we do take the welfare of our citizens very
seriously and that we will do our utmost to ensure that all of those
within our borders are protected.

The Prime Minister has commissioned me to investigate all instances of
disappearance and I will ensure that this investigation is thorough
and far-reaching.

I thank you again for bringing this to my attention.

Yours sincerely,

Rt. Hon. T. Brightwater

A letter from Lord Brightwater to a Mrs Gordon. It is said that it was her letter that prompted the
initial investigation *(Source: The Brightwater Archive)*

The Coat of Arms of Sleights Primary School, the site of Ghost Plane phenomena.

Above: Roger Mullins and unknown airman survey the landscape. *(From the Mullins collection)*
Below: A title card from the unseen MOD "Phenomena" film.

TOP SECRET

Property of the Ministry of Defence
and
Royal Air Force

RAF FYLINGDALES: 'PHENOMENA'

Creatures from the Meadow

The Ploughman's Wrath

The Ploughman's Wrath

Stanley Fullerton always had a passion for turnips. A moderately successful farmer of root crops, Stanley's expertise lay in the cultivation of magnificent and large turnips. When the judges spoke of his prize-winning efforts they celebrated the size and taste of these impressive specimens. His wife's turnip soup was the talk of the district. On competition day his wife and three children would wear hats fashioned from the shells of dried turnips. These would be decorated with dried flowers collected and pressed by his wife throughout the year. Fullerton experimented with the soil, spiking, irrigation methods and manure types whilst slavishly following advice from fellow farmers and farming journals. The result of this was that Fullerton's turnips were the talk of the village. No-one came close. He was the clear winner for five years running.

In the sixth year, hopes were high in the Fullerton household for another triumph. Sarah Fullerton had bought a new pot for her soup, the children were decorating their turnip headdresses and the crop was very impressive. Some turnips were the size of Stanley's head and a few bigger even than Squire Donnelly's (whose cranium was so abnormally large that he had to go to York to buy his hats from a specialist milliner.) So it was, with some surprise and trepidation that, on the eve of the competition, Sarah noticed her husband looking somewhat down in the mouth.

He did not laugh or clap when the children paraded in their turnip hats. He did not kiss his wife in welcome on his return from the field. He did not finish his meal, nor did he sup his ale.

His wife put this strange mood down to nervousness. But when she asked him how he was, he stared into space just above her head. When she kissed his cheek, he flinched as though irritated. And when she lay with him in their bed, he turned his back to her.

Sarah Fullerton awoke in the night to find her husband staring at the ceiling. When she enquired whether he had managed to get any sleep, he merely grunted and continued to stare. Sarah sat up, lighted a candle and insisted that "enough was enough", that he must "leave this dreadful daze" and tell her "what was what" or "who had done what to whom". She followed this by asking why he was "so maudlin" or how he had "fallen into such a darkness" and to stop his "moping, speak up" and start telling her what it was that was so bewitching him.

Stanley lowered his eyes. She commanded him to look at her. Reluctantly he returned her gaze.

"My turnips are inadequate," he said.

Sarah gasped, the shock she felt was akin to hearing a blasphemous curse from the mouth of a priest. Finally composed she spoke. "You will win tomorrow."

He nodded, "That I may do, but it will be a sorry lie. My turnips are miniscule, they are unimpressive. They are pathetic."

Sarah demanded that he tell her what had brought on this malaise.

156

And so Stanley sat up in bed and recounted how he had walked a different route across the moor that day. How he had happened upon a vast hole in the heather sinking far into the ground. How it was twenty yards wide and heaven knew how deep. He told her how he saw a ploughed field by this chasm with furrows so deep that when he walked in the ditch, the sides were up to his waist. How he found a crop of carrots each as long and wide as his arm. How he pulled up a potato the size of a new-born child. And he talked about the turnips. He talked of how he had found a turnip that he could only have carried with a wheelbarrow. A turnip so large that his head ached to think of it, his stomach rumbled and his envy grew.

Sarah's eyes grew wider with the telling, with every furrow and carrot and potato and turnip. Her mind raced. Cunning and guile rose up in her soul, a powerful tempting sensation that snuck in, raising its little head, before winding about her heart and making all become a delicious darkness. She smiled wide as her husband finished his tale. She pulled him close and stroked his worried head. She whispered plans into his ear and wrapped her own delicious darkness around his heart.

Two key phrases were said and repeated over and over that night.

The first was: "One for the prize."

The second: "One for the pot."

So it was with great excitement, mingled with terrible guilt and shame that Stanley Fullerton found himself out on the moor with his largest barrow. The field was utterly silent. Not a cricket chirped, nor an owl hooted. The air was still. The creak of the barrow wheel, the groan of wood, the step of guilty foot on soil, the squelch and scrape of spade in mud; all of these sounds echoed loud and angry across the moor. It took every ounce of strength to lift the turnip into the barrow and, as he rested, panting hard into the night, he thought he heard a strange wild snort, a vast breath, an enormous whinny echoing up from the depths of the earth. He stopped. Looking about into the dark, he waited a good minute for another sound, another strange loud breath, to give him an excuse to run. When nothing happened he sighed and began to work on the second, even larger turnip. Within an hour he was slowly pushing the grumbling barrow home to his wife.

As the sun rose for the annual Harvest Fair, few could imagine the excitement and delight that would erupt at the sight of the Fullerton turnip. Cake stalls were erected, coconut shies built and jars of sweets, chutney, pickles and jams laid out on trestle tables. Bunting of great variety and shade swept from stall to stall, across field and around marquee, in a dazzling dance of fluttering colour. The vegetables for judging were laid out. Stanley had put his turnip on a blanket, rather than on a table for fear that its weight would break the wood. To build a sense of anticipation Sarah advised him to hide the enormous turnip beneath a sheet. Sarah was busying herself at a cauldron. She had initially used an axe to break the turnip apart. She had been worried that the turnip would be tasteless and fibrous, but was delighted to discover it to be sweet, flavoursome and smooth. There would be enough soup to feed the entire village. She imagined the wives chattering and flocking to her for the recipe. The compliments, the gratitude, the invitations to dinner.

At eleven o'clock the band struck up. Their joyous brass echoed across the field. The Morris Men capered and the crier clanged his bell, calling out the order of events and encouraging all to sample wares, buy jam, drink ale, throw balls at coconuts imported from darkest India and more besides.

By quarter past eleven two very exciting things were starting to occur. Firstly, the vegetables were now available for inspection by the public and the judges. Whilst a few were impressed by David Grantchester's radishes, some cooed with admiration at William Smith's potatoes, and most expressed astonishment at the size of Bernard Tanner's marrow, all were struck into dumbfounded silence at Stanley Fullerton's turnip. A crowd gathered and did not move. Their reaction was akin to the unveiling of a new work by Rembrandt or a group of lads catching sight of a maiden bathing in a lake. The crowd was silent, reverent, and awestruck. Secondly, those who weren't gathered around Stanley's offering were queuing to get a bowl of Sarah's delicious soup. Those who had finished were keen to go back for more. They were happy to join the line again, to wait, to taste the perfect soup. Her three children gathered the pennies, counting them carefully before handing out bowls and spoons to the eager customers.

You would have thought that the other stall holders, Morris Men and band would have stood despondent, bereft of custom or attention. But, you would have found them either in the crowd around the turnip or in the line for Sarah's soup. Eventually, once he had drunk three bowls of soup and examined the turnip closely, the crier snapped from his reverie and called the Harvest Fair back into some semblance of normality. People drifted back to their stalls, Morris Men capered, the band tooted, coconuts tumbled from their cups and judges scribbled notes onto paper – desperately trying to keep their focus on the vegetable they were appraising, saving Stanley Fullerton's turnip until the very end.

How the crowd cheered at the mention of Sarah Fullerton's soup. How they roared when Stanley accepted the rosette for the sixth year running. His family hugged him tight, the children looking up at him with joy. His wife beamed out at the crowd, her eyes alive with pride, and her mind fighting back the now nagging doubt with bright indignation.

"He deserves this," she thought. "We deserve this. This is ours. I made the soup. He carried them. He dug them up. We worked for this. This is ours. This is ours."

Stanley Fullerton grinned too. But his eyes were dark. Guilt and shame consumed him. A shadow hung over his brow. He smiled and joked with the judges. He graciously accepted the compliments of the crowd and his competitors, but his words felt hollow, his laughter false.

"I do not deserve this," he thought. "We do not deserve this. This is not ours. She made the soup

160

from stolen ware. I carried the turnips. I dug them up. I did not ask. I did not work for this. This is not mine. This is not ours."

None of this worry was apparent to the crowd. Stanley carved the turnip with a heavy heart. He cut out an archway and seat so children could sit inside. After their larks were complete he sliced it into sections, handing them out to the crowd for free. His wife scowled at this but he silenced her with a whisper.

"I will take no money for this," he said.

And, after the moon rose over the stalls and the villagers went to their beds with their bellies full and their wagging tongues tired, Stanley and Sarah Fullerton lay awake staring at the ceiling. Stanley wallowing with guilt and Sarah fighting the shame with her own sense of entitlement.

"This is ours," she repeated over and over. "This is ours."

"This is not ours," thought Stanley, staring at the dark cracks in the plaster above his head. "This is not ours."

It rained that night. The water hammered down onto the roof making the possibility of sleep near impossible for Mr and Mrs Fullerton. When they stumbled out of bed the next morning, unsatisfied by their rest, Stanley would not talk to his wife. The children buzzed down into the kitchen chirruping, fluttering, squeaking and nattering. Their distracted brains did not notice the sour looks or heavy-lidded eyes of their parents. They cheeped outside and flew about the garden, jumping, skipping, tripping, scuffing knees, crying and laughing. None of their noise penetrated the cold silence that hung between Mr and Mrs Fullerton; not the bawling of their youngest that he had been pushed into a prickly shrub, nor the tugging on mother's sleeve for "please another glass of milk", nor the shouts for them both to come out and "look at this here puddle."

Stanley Fullerton turned his mug of cold tea in his hand.

"Look at the puddle, pa!"

Sarah Fullerton let the cold porridge drip from the end of her spoon back into the bowl.

"Ma, come see this puddle!"

Stanley Fullerton glared hard at his wife.

"Pa, it's right strange, this puddle!"

Sarah Fullerton took another scoop of porridge, raising it high to watch it slop back down in great dollops.

"Ma, the puddle! The puddle! Come and see the puddle!"

Hands pulled and pushed at their arms, their sleeves and their backs.

"Pa, you have to see this puddle. You have to!"

The children strained at the chairs, trying to pull their parents from the table.

"Puddle! Puddle! Puddle!"

Stanley and Sarah turned their glare from each other to their children and in an instant the dour spell was broken. All three children were hopping from foot to foot, grinning from ear to ear, shouting, pulling, dragging.

In a daze the Fullertons found themselves out in the mid-morning light, standing in the centre of the yard, looking down at a dark puddle of water. At least two feet wide, a sharp crescent shape.

"It's deep, Pa!" shouted the eldest, jumping in up to his knees.

Sarah scolded the boy. Stanley looked confused. He prided himself in keeping a level yard. The children were running around again, the eldest squelching and laughing at the discomfort of cold cloth against skin. Stanley sighed. He shifted some gravel from a pile by the shed, shovelling it into the hole until it was full. Sarah squinted at the shape.

"It's funny, but doesn't that look like…"

Her observation was interrupted by another shout.

"We found another!"

The parents ran to where their children stood. Looking down they saw a second puddle, the same strange C-shape about seven yards from the first.

"And another!"

Sure enough, about a further seven yards on was another puddle, the same shape as the last. The children now ran back and forth, finding more and more, running in two columns at regular intervals across the yard. Stanley Fullerton shook his head.

"I have never seen the like…" he stammered.

They followed the line of holes beyond the yard into the field. They could see the grass and brush broken where each puddle had formed. Stanley and Sarah glanced at each other. Neither of them wanted to voice what they thought might be the cause. They dared not speak it aloud. At the edge of the field leading into the village they could see the shattered remains of a dry stone wall exactly at the point where one of these puddles should have been. As they walked through the copse on the edge of the village they could see trees bent and torn, branches

163

hanging, trunks pulverised in the path of these mysterious holes.

The Harvest Fair was devastated. The marquee flattened, the tables crushed, the bunting torn and fluttering weakly on the drying mud. Sarah's cauldron was overturned, a large C-shaped dent in its side. And on the holes went, out of the Harvest Fair and into the village itself.

The poor village.

Houses sat forlorn, hatless; their roofs shattered, tiles scattered and smashed upon the road. Rain sodden rafters wept into rubble. Every house broken. Stones fallen. And everywhere these holes. Everywhere silence.

Stanley ran into Bernard Tanner's house, calling his name, whilst Sarah and the children waited outside. They could hear him scrabbling among the ruins, then, a strangled sob. His ashen face as he walked out of the battered house confirmed the worst.

It was the same in every house he was able to enter; the desperate search, the calling of names, and the inevitable shake of the head as he stumbled onto the street. Sarah was weeping uncontrollably and the older children joined her wailing. The youngest was confused, wondering why the game had finished. Suddenly she chirruped with delight.

"Horsie!"

Sarah turned to look in the direction that her daughter was pointing. The church stood at the end of the street. Untouched by the devastation. There was no horse. But there was something. Branches of a tree behind the tower swished in the wind. But the air was still. The branches moved again.

"Horsie!" squealed the youngest.

Sarah, Stanley and their three children edged down the street to get a closer look. The branches twisted and shifted again.

A great thud echoed across the village followed by another and another and another.

Thud. Thud. Thud.

Each one a thunder strike. Each one shaking the teeth. Wobbling the flesh. Beating the marrow.

Thud. Thud. Thud.

Thunder. Thunder. Thunder.

The Fullertons drew closer to the church. The branches of the trees on either side ripped and torn.

Stanley opened the church gate and stepped into the graveyard. He put his hand up to his mouth. Every gravestone was toppled and each grave lay open, clods of turf thrown hither and thither. Coffins within splintered. Corpses disinterred, broken and crushed.

Thunder. Thunder. Thunder.

Stanley pulled his family to him. His arms around each of them. Holding them tight as around the side of the church stalked an enormous Shire horse, its head level with the guttering of the nave. On its broad back sat a huge dark figure. Tree trunk arm outstretched, an enormous finger pointing down at the faces of the Fullertons.

Stanley Fullerton kissed his wife on the forehead and told his family to close their eyes. He would watch over them. He would protect them.

And so Stanley watched as the Shire horse, at its master's unspoken command, reared high into the air. Its hooves kicking at the stars before thundering down into flesh, bone and soil.

(This story has often been thought to help explain the huge circular marks that have been found near RAF Fylingdales. These marks resemble huge hoof prints and there is a variety of lore associated with them, from the tale of The Ploughman and his horse to the legend of the Bouncing Demon and the Soil of Death. These are tales that have a heavy resonance that still lasts to this day.)

Creatures from the Meadow

Song of the Meadow Bird

Song of the Meadow Bird

The dawn light breaks
My song will fly and shatter wings
In your giant arrow point you fly
I call you down from out the sky
Join my song, the song you've heard
The sweet song of the Meadow Bird

Midday sun shines
My song will soar and draw you close
Change your path and move your flight
Send you down into my night
Join my song, the song you've heard
The sweet song of the Meadow Bird

The twilight fades
My song will hold and pull you down
Into my heather you will fall
And with my own voice you will call
That lullaby, that song you've heard
The sweet song of the Meadow Bird

Creatures from the Meadow

The Ticking Policeman

The Ticking Policeman

Tick … tick.
Tick … tick.

Mary Salter lived in a sweet little cottage on the outskirts of the Black Meadow. The tiny dwelling, which consisted of only two rooms, the kitchen and her bedchamber, was her home from her birth in 1892 until her death in 1967. Her parents died when she was in her early twenties, she never married and found employment as a schoolteacher in Sleights. Her house stood on the edge of a small wood looking out across the vast mist-covered expanse of the North York Moors. Very little changed in that time, she did save up for a flushable toilet for her outhouse and by the mid 1950s had electric lights and a radio set. She still had her father's gramophone and never considered purchasing an electronic version. If you sat outside her house at night you could hear Verdi's *Requiem* or Pickering Brass playing out across the empty moor.

Tick … tick.
Tick … tick.

It was in the autumn of 1934 that her equilibrium was challenged. She had just finished marking a set of books when she heard a quiet ticking sound. She held her pocket watch to her ear, listening to its familiar panicked chattering rhythm before putting it down and lifting her head. It was most peculiar. The ticking appeared distinct, yet

177

distant. She got up from the kitchen table. The noise appeared louder as she approached the kitchen window. Slow but clear.

Tick ... tick.
Tick ... tick.

Tick followed ellipsis. Ellipsis followed tick.
Mary reached out. The window creaked open.

Tick ... tick.

Louder now but still distant. There was nothing for it. She put on her galoshes and stepped out into the evening.

Tick ... tick.

Mary Salter walked onto the moor. As she did so the sound grew fainter. She walked back towards the house and noted that the sound grew in volume. Mary giggled as she found herself remembering the childhood game.

"Warmer," she whispered.

She stepped to the side of the house.

Tick ... tick.

"Even warmer."

She moved away across the moor and noted that the sound was faint again.

"Colder."

Tick ... tick.

So Mary Salter walked to the back of the house.

Tick … tick.

"Hotter."

The sound was loud now. It was as though she were standing right next to the Grandfather clock in her empty classroom, its pendulum swinging back and forth. She stepped towards the wood.

Tick … tick.

"Boiling," she said.

Now she was inside the Grandfather clock itself. Watching the mechanism click through its business. Riding the pendulum like a merry-go-round steed. She stepped into the trees.

Tick …

The sound ceased. Mary Salter craned her neck to see what could be making that noise. It seemed so close now. She squinted into the dark. Branches obscured her vision. She scrutinised each black trunk, each mound and shape for any clue. Was there something there? She stood stock still. "Tick again," she thought. She was not frightened, instead rather sad that the old sound had stopped.

Then…

A snap of a twig…

A footfall…

Tick … tick.

Behind her now. She whipped round. Where was it? She thought she caught sight of movement around the side of the house. Mary Salter went to run, to see what it was, but was stopped by a new sound.

A smash of glass.

A slam of door.

Silence.

A faint ticking.

A scream.

Then...

Tick ... tick.

Without another thought Mary ran around to the front of her cottage. The glass pane in the door was smashed, the door hanging open. Poking from the doorway were the battered soles of two shoes. On closer inspection she saw that they were attached to the feet of an unkempt gentleman lying sprawled upon the floor. He was shaking uncontrollably. Around his head were coins and pound notes. On quick inspection Mary realised that these were her savings; the blue pot she kept them in lay in pieces on the floor.

The man struggled to his feet. His eyes wide and staring. He still had a sixpence in his hand. He held it out to her.

"Here..." he stammered. "Take it. He said I was to give it back."

Mary took the sixpence and eyed the man quizzically.

"Were you robbing me, young man?"

"Yes ma'am and I'm right sorry."

"I want you out of my house."

"Of course ma'am - but he said to wait here whilst I wait for the constabulary."

"You will not run?"

"He advised that I do not. So I will not ma'am."

Mary Salter was perplexed by this.

"What is your name?"

"Ernie Halfcoat, ma'am."

"Ernie Halfcoat? Earnest Halfcoat?"

"Aye."

"I thought I taught you better than this Earnest."

"I know ma'am. Sorry ma'am. If I'd known it was you who lived here..."

"Earnest Halfcoat, I trust that you would have learnt not to thieve or rob from *anyone*."

"Yes ma'am."

"Well then, you pick up my savings and count them out for me on the table. Then put them in this tin. I'll make us a nice cup of tea."

At the sink she filled up the bottle, looking out of the window into the woods behind the house. A figure stood in front of the trees. As still as stone. A tall black hat on its head, shining black moustache, sharp tailored long-coat and breeches and a stout night-stick in gloved hand. Stiffly, and with jerky movements, it raised its hand to its hat, doffing it to Mary Salter before turning and striding into the woods. The sound of ticking grew fainter and fainter until it vanished.

Mary put the kettle on the hob. She turned to Earnest Halfcoat who was diligently counting out the money as she had ordered.

"Well my guardian angel has gone," she said.

Earnest grunted. "No 'e 'asn't."

"I'm sorry? But whoever he was he protected me."

"He's protecting me, ma'am."

"He's protecting you? From what?"

"From me own mischief."

Mary Salter sat down wearily at the table. Earnest tutted and began to count coins again.

"Arithmetic was never one of your strong points Earnest. Would you like me to…"

"No ma'am. I'd like to get sommat right for once. Hadn't you better call for the constable?"

"How? I have no telephone."

"It's only a short walk to the nearest box, ma'am."

Mary Salter laughed. "Earnest Halfcoat, if you think I am going to leave you here on your own with my savings!"

"I must make amends, ma'am. I promise you I will not thieve from you…" Mary Salter squinted at Earnest Halfcoat. "…or anyone else ever again."

She shook her head. "I'm sorry, Earnest but I am afraid that even my trust and good nature fail to stretch that far."

Tick … tick.
Tick … tick.

The kettle whistled. As she poured boiling water into the teapot, letting it steep in silence, she heard the ticking again. Growing louder and louder.

Tick … tick.

The latch of the front door lifted.

Tick ... tick.

The hinges creaked.

Tick ... tick.

There, bathed in moonlight, stood the same figure as before.

Tick ... tick.

Earnest looked up, tutted and began to count again.

Tick ... tick.

The figure lifted his hat to Mary. She could see his smooth cream tin face, rivets running from ear to chin, shining boot-black tin moustache and painted kind tin eyes. With a creak of metal and a grind of gears he turned, raising his hand, encouraging her to leave the cottage.

Tick ... tick.

Earnest tutted again.
"Looks like I'm not going anywhere," he said.
Mary Salter grabbed her coat and hat and made for the telephone box.
The ticking policeman stood at the door.
Earnest Halfcoat began to count again.

Tick ... tick.
Tick ... tick.

Tick ... tick.
Tick ... tick.
Tick ... tick.

(This tale is based on a transcript of conversation between Roger Mullins and the successful retired accountant E. Halfcoat in 1968.)

Creatures from the Meadow

March of the Meadow Hags

March of the Meadow Hags

"We fear the Pear tree."
"So old, so large with long branches, weighed down
with black and pink fruits."
"Poison."
"Beneath the tree sits an ancient well, filled in by
the farmer who used to own this land."
"The pears grow but do not drop."
"They sit and suck at the rich earth."
"Flies buzz about their stench."
"They are more fungi than fruit."
"At sunset you can see the shadow of the pear tree.
Its vast spindly claws scratching at the scarlet
sky."
"Its fruit like cankers on every branch."
"We fear the pear tree. But most of all we fear the
pears."

*(A selection of phrases taken from Roger Mullins'
"Pear Notes".)*

"I bit into a pear once and tasted nothing but blood
and gristle."

*(From a conversation with an old man by Stanley
Coulton.)*

The spring had been wet and the summer the
perfect mix of shower and sun. Tom the Gatekeeper,

had asked me to take a look at the pear tree in the lower field. I was rather surprised at this. Tree husbandry was not my area of expertise. I had only recently purchased the land and had other concerns; with the house and drainage rather than a musty old pear tree. I had little love for pears anyway. I find the flesh gritty and the flavour has been known to make me retch. However I am partial to chilled pear cider. Life often throws up these strange little conundrums. I promised Tom that I would go with him but was called away on business to India. Oddly while I was staying with the Hungarian Ambassador in Delhi a few weeks later I received a letter from Tom, the gist of which was that he was deeply concerned about this damnedly strange tree, it was causing him all sorts of bother. Something about roots and the stench if I recall. I sent a letter back, instructing him to chop the damned thing down. I didn't hear another peep from Tom but on my return was informed that he hadn't been seen for some time. We assumed that he had grown tired of the estate and had moved elsewhere. Funny thing was, one of the other labourers said that the pear tree was still there and that he had been talking to the local priest about cutting it down himself. I assumed that Tom had not received my letter. This was all academic as a fantastic property became available in Norfolk, so I quickly sold up and thought no more about it.

(From "Sculpting the Horizon" – Memoirs of a Victorian Landowner by Viscount Walter Cavendish).

When the pear drops down
Don't smile or frown.
Take a deep breath
Run fast from death.

When the pear hits soil
The skin will boil,
Shiver and crack.
Run. Don't look back.

(Child's rhyme taken from a school book found in 1935 by the Brightwater Team.)

I bloody hate pears.

(William Smith in conversation with Sir Stanley Coulton - June 1872)

And so it is the unnatural that the Devil will put before us. We must think on that which is good and pure and natural. There are those that tempt us with the new, the strange and the exotic. But I say to you, no. We shall not look. We will stay away. We shall turn our backs. When the devil comes before me do I let him in? No. "Get thee behind me Satan," we shout out. We let him know who is master. When he tempts us with the strange and the new. Do we embrace it? No. We say "Get thee behind me Satan."

Our young folk are tempted by the new. They gather on the fields, they cavort, they play their music and dance to the pagan beat of a drum, they visit the strange old pear tree with its engorged unnatural fruit. They dare each other to climb, to pluck down one of those pears that should have so easily fallen upon the dirt. But they do not fall. No pulling will bring them down for they are not of nature. They are not of God. And the children dance and jeer.

It was only last Saturday that I happened upon a group of your children dancing about the pear tree. And where were you? Why was it I who warned them from that unholy site? And would they come willingly? No. Not until I had broken their drum. Not until I had beaten and cudgelled their leader. Not until I had snapped their flutes and stamped upon their penny whistles. Not until I had commanded the girls to roll down their sleeves, tie up their wild hair and put their hats upon their naked heads.

And they are here today. Kneeling in supplication and begging forgiveness for their transgressions. And, I say unto you. Look upon the cross. Look upon God. Let not your eye wander to the new and the strange. Let not your heart be stolen. Let not your mind be turned. Let all your thoughts be on God and his wonders and not upon the Devil and his works.

(Taken from a Sermon by Reverend Stanthorpe in "Collected Sermons from the Moors" – The third Appendix to "Inside the Victorian mind" by Professor R. Fletchley – Cambridge University Press 1957)

I hav had too bye anuther sor. The won I had
        witch I thort was strong is bluntd. The
teeth hav all broak of. Yu wil need too bye
an ax hed to. It shaterd wen it hit the
trunk. I tride the othur and that broak to.
I now hav no axs nor do I hav a wurkin sor.
I wil cum by on the murrow too collect som
    munny too by a nue sore and too nue axs.
        I did not mak a dent. Thank yue.

*(A note discovered in Reverend Stanthorpe's diaries.
There is no date or indication when it was written.)*

A pear is ripe and ready to drop in late August or
early September depending on the temperature and
humidity. You may see them on the tree as late as
November in certain circumstances but they will be
wrinkled and unwilling to drop. It is, however,
improbable that a pear would sit on a branch until
the following spring unless, I suppose, it is frozen
for all of that time. However, in response to your
initial query, for a pear or a group of pears to
continue growing through the winter into the
following spring and summer is the stuff of fiction.
It is a whimsical thought and while I enjoy the
momentary diversion of considering such absurdity,
I hope you will forgive that I spend no further time
on answering your most amusing question.

*(Extract from a letter from Professor Bernard
Hartleton of the Royal Horticultural Society to Simon
Walters, Schoolmaster of Sleights School. 1895)*

Thank yu for the munny too by a nue ax. I
was abl to by too. I was told that th ax wos
of a vary strong ion. It wos all so vary
sharp. How ever it broak on the second
stroak. I did not triy too yous the nue
sore. I think yu need to triy sumthing els.

(A second note discovered in Reverend Stanthorpe's diaries. Once again it is not dated.)

Take an old branch
Dry and brittle
Pile up the sticks
Big and little
Around the trunk
Around the stem
Around the pear tree's
Smooth bark hem
Pile up the kindling
Pile it high
As high as the pears
That shadow the sky
Dance with the torches
Smile and sing
Run round the flames
In dancing ring
Laugh as the flames
Climb up so high
Lick at the pears
That shadow the sky

(Anonymous rhyme discovered by Sir Stanley Coulton as recorded in "Pickering Walks" - 1895)

The Reverend was rather shaken up when we found him. His cassock was torn, his hair in disarray. I had been speaking to my constable when we heard about the conflagration.

The Reverend Stanthorpe and about twenty members of his congregation had made their way onto the moors to the old pear tree. It was a strange thing that tree. Only patches of heather and bramble in a very dry condition and yet amidst all that was this tree. We were surprised when we got down there to find a massive blaze about the tree. The large fruit seemed to sizzle and pop, blackened in the smoke, but no branch or pear fell. This was a surprise as the fruit were far too large for each branch that they hung upon. We counted thirteen fruit, each of them appeared to be the size of a small child's head. We gathered up the parishioners and bade them come with us to the town so that they would do themselves no more mischief. So caught up as they were in the frenzy of fire and raucous hymn-singing. They all came quietly except the Reverend who insisted on staying.

When we tried to lay hands upon him to move him on he shook us off, shouting that the tree must be destroyed and its devil fruit with it. He said he would "see it through". He ran off into the dark and we could not see where he had gone. Once the rest of his followers were safely back in their homes the sun was rising so we went to look for him again.

The tree was bare. Black and twisted against the rising sun. We found the Reverend pale and shaking, mumbling in the dawn light nonsense about "pears, ash and women". We could make head

nor tail of it so naturally took him to the local
sanatorium at Pickering.

*(Taken from an interview with retired Constable
Stanley Butterworth of Whitby and Pickering 1894)*

Thirteen ripe pears hanging on a tree
Count them, count them, one, two, three
Twirl and turn
Watch it burn
The branch loses grip, a pear drops free
She rises from the ash for all to see

Twelve ripe pears hanging on a tree
Count them, count them, one, two, three
Twirl and turn
Watch it burn
The branch loses grip, a pear drops free
She rises from the ash for all to see

Eleven ripe pears hanging on a tree
Count them, count them, one, two, three
Twirl and turn
Watch it burn
The branch loses grip, a pear drops free
She rises from the ash for all to see

Ten ripe pears hanging on a tree
Count them, count them, one, two, three
Twirl and turn
Watch it burn
The branch loses grip, a pear drops free
She rises from the ash for all to see

Nine ripe pears hanging on a tree
Count them, count them, one, two, three
Twirl and turn
Watch it burn
The branch loses grip, a pear drops free
She rises from the ash for all to see

Eight ripe pears hanging on a tree
Count them, count them, one, two, three
Twirl and turn
Watch it burn
The branch loses grip, a pear drops free
She rises from the ash for all to see

Seven ripe pears hanging on a tree
Count them, count them, one, two, three
Twirl and turn
Watch it burn
The branch loses grip, a pear drops free
She rises from the ash for all to see

Six ripe pears hanging on a tree
Count them, count them, one, two, three
Twirl and turn
Watch it burn
The branch loses grip, a pear drops free
She rises from the ash for all to see

Five ripe pears hanging on a tree
Count them, count them, one, two, three
Twirl and turn
Watch it burn
The branch loses grip, a pear drops free
She rises from the ash for all to see

Four ripe pears hanging on a tree
Count them, count them, one, two, three
Twirl and turn
Watch it burn
The branch loses grip, a pear drops free
She rises from the ash for all to see

Three ripe pears hanging on a tree
Count them, count them, one, two, three
Twirl and turn
Watch it burn
The branch loses grip, a pear drops free
She rises from the ash for all to see

Two ripe pears hanging on a tree
Count them, count them, one, two...
Twirl and turn
Watch it burn
The branch loses grip, a pear drops free
She rises from the ash for all to see

One ripe pear hanging on a tree
Count it, count it, one ...
Twirl and turn
Watch it burn
The branch loses grip, a pear drops free
She rises from the ash for all to see

Thirteen old women under the tree
Count them, count them, one, two, three
Turn and turn
Burn and burn
The branches are empty, the pears are free
They step from the ash for you and me.

(Song of the thirteen pears – Popular children's rhyme collected by Sir Stanley Coulton in "Pickering Walks" – 1895)

Monday 15th October 1893

Patient 17 still non-responsive
Not taking food.
Drink is forced. Swallowed.
Occasional muttering but incomprehensible.

Tuesday 16th October 1893

Patient 17 still non-responsive.
Force fed gruel.
Drink forced. Swallowed.
Muttering. Phrases recorded.
"They come." "Village." "Village." "They come."

Wednesday 17th October 1893

Patient 17 responsive.
Allowed self to be fed.
Able to drink unaided.

Muttering. No direct conversation. Phrases recorded.

"Warn." "Warn." "Too late." "Too late." "Close the windows." "Do not accept help." "If help is offered do not accept it." "Close the windows"

Tuesday 18th October 1893

Patient 17 completely lucid.
Feeds self.
Drinks unaided.
Converses. Questions asked regarding recorded phrases.
Patient puzzled at them.
Fugue state suggested.
Monitoring.

Friday 19th October 1893

Patient 17 released.
Constabulary to monitor.
Fugue state recorded.
Patient 17 very coherent, intelligent, calm.
No indication of previous condition presented.
Suggestion: exposure on moor lead to hypothermia, symptoms including hallucinations and temporary psychosis.

(Records from Pickering Sanatorium – Doctor Julius Pargiter – taken from the Brightwater Archive.)

Great Uncle Earnest was a traditional sort. He had a big farm, as mother told me, and a large family. He and his wife had struggled to produce boys. There were two of them: Daniel and Michael and eleven daughters. None of them were taken early as was so common in those days. The eleven daughters were a real handful. When he had the time to visit *The Plough* in Sleights he would moan and moan at "them awful girls". They wouldn't lift a finger and their mother, that harridan, that witch, that bitch (as grandma used to call her), that hussy. She would encourage them to belittle him, to shirk and leave all the work to him and his boys. Edna, my great Aunt, had married beneath her, it was said, and she demanded that he kept her in the style she had become accustomed to. Though he kept a lot of land and his business thrived, he could not afford a maid and so the household chores and the cleaning and the pandering after Edna and her eleven daughters was left to Earnest and his two hard-working sons.

It was a strange state of affairs – a reversal of the usual one might say. But he loved her and his daughters even though he cursed their names, the days they were born and the day he was wed.

According to Grandma, his complaints were not unfounded. For no more ungrateful, foul-mouthed, lazy bunch of girls had she ever met. She rarely visited her brother for she found the experience draining in the extreme. How she pitied those poor sons. She prayed that the girls would see the error of their ways, they would relent from their selfishness. She had seen the youngest, Beth and Amelia running around their father as he cooked the evening meal. She had witnessed Edna sitting with

201

her feet on the pouffe, reading a penny dreadful, whilst three daughters Millicent, Jemima and Gwendolen played at cribbage. Two of the elder daughters put themselves about most improperly and it was a constant source of relief to Eric that he didn't find himself a Grandfather to Emily and Anna's bastard offspring. However the shame caused by their behaviour took its toll and he became increasingly cantankerous. No more so than when Tabitha, Samantha, Sarah and Ruth were expelled for fighting with some boys in their class. Grandma has only seen Ernest cry on two occasions. The first was with rage and shame on the retelling of his encounter with the schoolmistress.

She could not see how things could change as the influence of Edna was so great. The girls were encouraged to demand and to behave without the decorum expected of a real lady. But, that said, despite his complaints, he did love them. He would be the first to defend his eldest daughters, with fists if necessary, when a drunkard named them as whores or tarts. "They are my daughters," he would shout. He would love them whatever, whether sinful or pure.

(Taken from a conversation between Claire Stott and Roger Mullins, recorded in May 1965.)

Well, lots of folk talked of seeing the old women on the moor. They walked together, in time, holding hands, sweeping across the heather with the mist. They could often be seen at dawn. People gave them a wide berth. So strange they looked. Dark ragged shawls, faces so wrinkled. They could have been sisters they looked so alike but they all seemed of the same age, so they could not be. It was a sight to see them with the morning sun behind their backs looking down at the village from the hill.

(Taken from a conversation between Roger Mullins and Thomas Stokes in April 1962)

Monday 5ᵗʰ November 1893

Patient 17 has been returned by the constabulary due to complaints from Earnest Trentwood, a local farmer. Time of return four o'clock in the afternoon.
Lucid and taking food and drink.
However it appears from interview that Patient 17 is suffering some form of delusion.
Transcript of interview:
"Found them. Found them. Didn't see me. I stood behind a tree. They were still. Looking down at the Trentwood Farm. Holding hands. So still. Black rags in the wind. Turned to look at where I was. Held still. Black rags twisting towards me. Closed my eyes. When I opened them again. They'd gone. Down the hill. To the farm."

(Records from Pickering Sanatorium – Doctor Julius Pargiter – Taken from The Brightwater Archive)

Shadows in the sun
Black against the sky
Down hill, down hill down
Feet tramp heather
Black hessian fly
Down hill, down hill down

Over hill through bramble deep
Over hardy stone
Past the livestock fast asleep
To heart and hearth and home

Shadows on the moor
Ragged raggy sigh
Down hill, down hill down
Feel your hearts in chill
As thirteen voices cry
Down hill, down hill down

Rapping on your door they come
Lonely in the cold
A plaintive cry to let them in
Through door, to your threshold

*(Lyrics of a song recorded by Roger Mullins in 1962 –
in his notes he indicates that the singer was called
Abigail Morley and that the song was "slow and
mournful")*

A Perfect Wife

Washes up

Is silent unless asked to speak
Will embrace at husband's need
Will fetch whatever is asked for -
      The pipe
      The slippers
      The socks
      The shoes
Will pick up after the husband
Will wash the children
Read the children their story
Will love even where love is not returned
Love honour and obey

<u>A Perfect Daughter</u>

Will agree
Will not answer back
Will dress in long hem and not show the ankle let
alone the shin
Will come when called
Will knit
Will sew
Will arrange the flowers from the meadow
Will be everything the father wants
Will obey the brothers
Will sing beautifully
Will not sigh or pout or groan or stamp or moan or
growl or flounce

*(Taken from a printed tea-towel bought from the
Ryedale Folk Museum in 1961 – it is said to have
been written by a local farmer's wife when asked to
lay down the secrets of her happy family.)*

Monday 5th November 1893

Transcript continues:
"I know I shouldn't have done, but I followed
them to the farm. I kept my distance. They
never once turned about. Never once. The
farmer and his two sons were in the field,
hard at work on the soil. I wanted to call
out. But I feared for myself. The thirteen
women, the thirteen hags from the tree, for
that is who they were, stopped for a moment
and turned their heads to the field. They all
turned their heads at precisely the same
moment. A mechanical movement. Like the
clockwork creatures at the penny arcade.
Click. Turn Click. Turn back. Down the hill
to the farm. Black hessian fluttering, like
raven wings.

They reached the yard where three of the
youngest girls were running about. I
remember one of the old women let out a
screech, somewhere between a bark and a
scream. The girls stopped. The old woman who
had made this appalling noise cocked her
head to one side and scrutinised the three
girls who now stood shocked into mute
stillness. She spoke, her voice dusty with
age.
"Why are you playing when there is work to
be done?"
The children looked at each other. One of
them managed to giggle. The other two smiled,

but only for a moment, for the thirteen swept around them in a tight circle. The little girls screamed. Such terror. There was a loud crack and the screaming was replaced by the sound of two girls whimpering.

I could take no more. I sprang from behind the wall and ran forward. There was another snap and now only one child cried. I grasped the shoulders of two of the old ladies to pull them apart. They would not budge. They were as solid as stone. I craned my neck and saw the youngest daughter huddled on the floor next to the lifeless forms of her two sisters. Two hands snaked out from the circle growing with unnatural speed. Ivy fingers wrapped around the little girl's face then... a twist, a snap, a slump. The circle grew smaller. Three hags stepped into the centre. Climbing out of their black hessian rags, standing wrinkled and bare above the poor little corpses. Each hag crouched over a body. I could see. No. I am not certain, but I am sure that one of them was putting her hand inside the mouth of the little corpse and rooting around like a ragamuffin at a Country Fair Lucky Dip. I could see the elbow moving about, rotating, the hand moving up into the skull. Then it stopped. The arm withdrew with a squelch. The other two hags must have been doing the same with their prey as three hands shot into the air, each holding a pinkish, grey and bloodied round mass. Then as I watched, speechless, gagging, each crouching hag opened its mouth wide and swallowed the little brains in one gulp.

I could not tear my eyes away. I continued to push and pull at the immovable shoulders. I screamed and yelled, drawing the other girls and the farmer's wife out of the house. The farmer's wife was yawning, standing in her nightdress. Three daughters stood with playing cards still in their hands. Five more appeared at windows and doorways. I shouted at them to help and they ran forward. The hags parted, revealing the three daughters standing smiling.
"Mother," they said, in unison, holding out their hands to the farmer's wife.
Of the three naked hags there was no sign.

The farmer's wife looked puzzled. She asked the ten remaining women who they were and what they wanted. No-one answered. The hags all cocked their heads, studying the farmer's wife and her daughters with keen interest. The three little girls, who I had seen killed, stepped towards me. One grabbed my left hand, the other my right. The third raised her hand and placed it on my chest, looking up into my eyes. The hags suddenly flew in different directions. One towards the farmer's wife - eight to the remaining daughters. Leaving one. Silent. Watching me. There were screams and cracks. I tried to move, to help, but the little girls held me fast. And I saw. Oh God help me... I saw such things... such devilry... tearing... swallowing.

The farmer's wife and her daughters lay still. Scarlet smeared the mouths of the naked hags crouching over them. With a horrendous cracking of bones each hag diminished - they... shrank - smaller and smaller - until they were the size of a small child, a cat, a mouse. Once that size each tiny hag crawled inside the mouths of the dead. A moment passed. The farmer's wife blinked her eyes, sat up and smiled. The other daughters all did the same. The remaining hag looked at me. I felt hands release me. The three children stepped away.

The farmer's wife opened her mouth and shut it again. She continued to smile. "Time to get the washing in," she said.

One daughter picked up a broom and began to sweep the yard. Another collected the dropped playing cards together saying that they would do well for their brothers that evening. Others grabbed hoes, wheelbarrows and spades and went to join their father and brothers at work on the fields.

The hag cocked her head to one side and scrutinised me slowly.

I fled. God help me. I did not look back. Is she here? Is she outside? Is she outside?

Claire Stott: But things changed. He was rarely seen at the tavern now. Grandma's visits were far more frequent as she said that the whole experience was far more agreeable now. Those girls knew their place. They were demure. They were graceful. They were polite. They did not answer back. They did their chores. In fact it was the two brothers who appeared more lazy. For a while Grandma thought that this was well deserved as they had worked so hard but after a while their attitude grated. So used now were they to be being waited on hand and foot by their mother, the now charming Edna, and those daughters. Each grew to be a fine and helpful member of the community. Each took a husband – husbands who seemed satisfied and, uncommon in those days, those husbands did not stray, did not take a mistress. Just like my Great Uncle, (who, before this change, would never have been blamed for sowing his oats in another field), they were satisfied, happy that all was as it should be, everything in its place.

Roger Mullins: What do you think had caused this change?

Claire Stott: Well it was a strange and, according to Grandma, an almost overnight change. She assumed they had found religion. Indeed the local reverend was often around the house. He called

Edna and her daughters his "sisters", something which struck Grandma as strange. That said, there was not a more pleasant and kind gentleman she had ever met. He was as helpful as the girls, selfless and kind.

(Taken from a conversation between Claire Stott and Roger Mullins, recorded in May 1965.)

Wednesday 7th November 1893

Since the visit from his grandmother yesterday Patient 17 is a changed man. He scoffs at his earlier behaviour and is deeply apologetic for the disruption he has caused.

This is a most strange turn of events and so we will keep him under observation for a few more days. This is considered necessary after his vivid and disturbing account of the incident he claims to have witnessed. Also, considering the violent reaction on hearing that his grandmother had come to the sanatorium, it is vital that monitoring continues. He insisted that his grandmother lives in London and is far too frail to visit and so it could not be her.

She was indeed very frail and dressed in a black hessian cloak. When she arrived he had been sedated due to the violence of his reaction to the news of her arrival. We took her to his room. She asked if she could sit with him. We allowed this and left her alone. When the nurse went to check on him some hours later Patient 17's grandmother had left. The patient's demeanour had entirely changed. Perhaps a visit from his grandmother was just the tonic he needed.

Still we will continue to keep him under observation.

Friday 9th November 1893

Patient 17 was released today.
He assured us that we would have no further problems from him and that he was keen to go and visit his sisters.

(Records from Pickering Sanatorium – Doctor Julius Pargiter – Taken from The Brightwater Archive)

Creatures from the Meadow

The Maiden of the Mist

The Maiden of the Mist

As he lay on his back the sky shifted. The bright blue creaked into a mix of grey and white as the clouds invaded the endless sea above. The grass beneath his hands was warm and tender to his caressing fingers. He was aware of the buzz of insects and the distant hum of the village, but from his vantage – lying still with nothing but sky for company, he felt blissfully alone.

She was gone.

She had been gone a long while. He lay on the spot where they had embraced in the breeze. Where the grass had been their bower. Where bodies met and life had sprung.

Blue peeked tantalisingly through wisps of soft white cotton.

She had asked him here for a picnic all those years ago. They had sat and giggled at his foolish master and her foolish students.

She had been gone a long while.

She had made sandwiches and he had brought strawberries. She let him feed them to her and giggled when the juice trickled down her chin.

He thought that one cloud looked just like a strawberry. Narrow at the bottom and wide at the top. A wisp of leaf and stalk. Most odd. It distorted slightly. A shift in the surface. Jagged. No longer smooth down one side. Little indentations appeared. Almost like a bite. He grinned. The juice had trickled down her chin.

She was gone.

She had been gone a long while.

He had tried to propose to her here. It was already their favourite spot. She had giggled when he went down on one knee and knelt down facing him. As he formed the question she said it at exactly the same time. As he responded in the positive, so did she.

He peered up. Two figures kneeling? It looked like that. A cloud with two heads and a gap between. Heads moving closer together, bobbing and weaving, becoming one.

She was gone.

She had been gone a long while.

Here her bare legs had brushed against the clover. Here her breath in his ear, a whisper of love, an intake of breath, a murmur. Here her hand on his. Her lips on his. Her heart with his. Here. It was here.

A face with dark brows glared down. Eyes staring and shifting in the eddies and flows of the wind. A mouth partly formed opened to a surprised "O" before widening into blue.

He turned his head from the clouds.

She was gone.

She had been gone a long while.

He had watched her chasing their son over the grass as he was pulled by the power of the kite. He had laughed with them as they rolled down the slope – last one to the bottom a rotten egg. When his son was older, almost a man, his smile diminished but he was still able to stare upwards. He was still willing to see more than simple shapes in the clouds. Did he still do that now? Was he lying on a hill somewhere making stories? Looking up? Would he share this with his wife, with his children?

His hand found the old china pot. He didn't want to look. The clouds danced. He would watch the clouds instead.

A range of mountains. Dark forbidding ranges with bright snow-capped peaks glowing from the sun behind. Shifting. A river running between the peaks down into the rift. A valley of dark grey swirling and spinning into a smile. A nose above, lips parted, eyes opening slow and wide. Drifting away out of vision.

He could feel the lid beneath his fingers. He didn't want to look. He played with the handle. Daring himself to lift it.

A tree. Two trees. A clump, a copse, a forest. Building, dancing, turning. A landscape. Hills, rivers, valley, pits, holes, swamps. A body. A body now. Lying in profile. Legs slightly crossed. The wave of hip – the stomach – the belly, breasts, neck and face – hair sweeping back – flowing into mist, into blue, into nothing.

Blue.

He searched the sky from east to west. The lovely unbroken blue.

His hand was lifting the lid. He sat up slowly, lifting the pot into his lap. Glancing down, for only a moment, the pot seemed so drab, so unimportant. Knees cracking, he rose to his feet, vague strands of hair writhing wild on his pitted scalp, whipped into geriatric frenzy by the unforgiving wind. He lifted the lid, tilting the pot into the mouth of the breeze. Grey tumbled into the sky, into the blue, a cloud.

She was gone.

The sky shifted.

He replaced the lid, lowered himself to the ground and lay on his back.

A bank of grey and white drifted from the west. Blank at first. A canvas of possibilities shifting into focus. Another face formed. Lips, teeth, tongue, nose and eyes wide, unmoving. A defined chin. A wisp of hair. The right eye winked. He shook his head, rubbing his hand over his eyes.

The face stared down at him. He reached up his hand to trace the contours, so defined and clear. He stopped. His hand had disturbed the cloud. Breaking its pattern. Breaking it apart. The cloud was only a few feet above him. He could feel its damp cold against his skin. The face swirled back into shape. He glanced down from the eyes of this maiden of mist and was astounded to see her neck, shoulders, arms, hands, chest, stomach, hips, thighs, knees, calves and feet all formed from swirling smoke. The figure smiled. He grinned back nervously. A misty hand drifted down before his eyes. Palm open. He sat up. Resting on the cloud palm were grains of grey ash. He looked into the maiden's face. She smiled again, her eyes flicking to the china pot at his side. She closed her palm into a fist, opening it again to reveal the ash gone. He looked closer. It was not gone. Not quite. The particles of ash now had lost some of their grey. But he could still see them. He reached out a finger to touch them, watching in surprise as they eddied and spun. Formless. Part of the cloud.

He looked back into her face.

She turned her head to the sky. Her mist hand drifted to point at a hill formed of cloud. Sitting high on the swirling bank, a figure looked up, watching the sky above her. Watching the tiny wisps of distant cloud skimming the edges of the atmosphere.

The Maiden of the Mist drifted her face back to his, smiling. Always smiling.

She reached out a fog hand to touch his cheek.

He could feel the dewy cold of her touch but that seemed to dissipate. His skin cooled to match her temperature. He moved his own hand to find hers and found his hand passing through hers and through his own mist-like cheek. He looked down. His hand, once solid, now drifted before his face in eddies and swirls. His clothes flopped untidily to the floor, no longer hanging on his aging skin, flesh and bone.

He sat. A cloud man on a hill.

The Maiden of the Mist held out her hand. He took it and they rose slowly into the sky. A dance of fog and mist.

He was gone.

*   *   *

They had sat there a long while. The earth seemed formless and swirling to them, but here, on this cloud, everything seemed vivid and real.

He felt his wife's hand in his. And the cloud swept and swirled into a new shape.

20th Century Encounters

The Audire

The Audire

When Mr Barrett first approached Roger Mullins to ask for information about the Brightwater Archive[3] I was unsurprised to learn that Mullins was not only unimpressed but very reluctant to help. He had fought the government to open the archive and he was not prepared to share his sensitive findings with anyone. Mullins was nonplussed by Barrett's celebrity. At that time (in 1967) Barrett was making waves with his new band at UFO[4] but Mullins was very sniffy about "junkies trying to open the doors of perception."[5] However, Mr Barrett managed to

---

[3] *The Brightwater Archive* is an extensive collection of files gathered by Lord Brightwater and his team when he investigated the disappearances on the North York Moors in the 1930s. After his investigation was closed down, due to a lack of funding, the files were locked away. They were briefly re-opened for the University of York when Roger Mullins was conducting his research in the 1960s and '70s. In 2013 the archive was opened again and elements of it are available to see online at thebrightwaterarchive.wordpress.com.

[4] *UFO* was a nightclub in London run by Joe Boyd and John Hopkins. The first bands to play there were *Soft Machine* and Syd Barrett's own *Pink Floyd*.

[5] Taken from Mullins' personal diaries – these are currently unpublished. The full quotation is found in an entry dated 5th March 1967 which is the day Barrett first approached Mullins at the University of York. "*The gentleman was unkempt with dark eyes and a mess of black scraggy hair. He appeared to me to be the sort of man who was looking for another "experience". I really have very little time for these junkies*

persuade Mullins, who showed him some key features of the archive that are, even now, blocked from public view. Mr Barrett himself never spoke of the archive publically and it would seem that his later isolation enabled him to take any secrets that Mullins shared to the grave.

When I asked Mullins what had changed his mind he told me that Mr Barrett had shared a story that Mullins had considered so useful that he was happy to give Barrett access to information relating to the land spheres[6], time slips[7], standing stones[8] and the disappearing village[9]. Barrett was reportedly also

---

trying to open the doors of perception. Why take hallucinogens when you have the Black Meadow to explore?"

[6] The Land Spheres have a very rich history of folklore attached to them. Giant black spheres were seen to float across the North York Moors on "Black Nights", their origin was unknown. Sightings diminished when the RAF constructed the "early warning system" Radomes on the moors.

[7] Many who have walked the moors have reported incidences of missing time. Several folk tales allude to this. "The Coalman and the Creature" and "The Long Walk to Scarry Wood" explore the notion of time travel long before it was fashionable to do so.

[8] There are many standing stones on the North York Moors. On the Black Meadow there is said to be a stone that is covered in arcane spirals that can be used for occult purposes.

[9] The Disappearing Village is the most significant and prolific part of Black Meadow folklore. It is said that a lost village appears and disappears when the mist is high:

"When the mist spreads
Like an unspooling ball of wool
Threading over the land
Can you see the smoke from the chimneys?

very interested in the tales that Mullins had been collecting. Mullins added Barrett's own account to his collection of notes which I am very pleased to be able to publish for the first time.

There is a strange link between Barrett and Mullins. Both were searching for something, both had grand obsessions and both disappeared; Barrett from the public eye and Mullins into the mist.

Professor Philip Hull – University of York - 2007

There was a singer who visited the Black Meadow. He was something of a celebrity, from the flatlands to the east of the country, whose songs smacked of a delicious Englishness that the folk singers of the moors would have embraced.

Mr Barrett, like many artists before him, was drawn to the mysteries of the North York Moors. What is it about this place that calls so many into its fog- ridden heart? He was looking for inspiration to help create a set of songs for his new band. He stayed the night at an inn in Sleights where he had a peaceful stay (as no-one knew who he was). In the early morning of a Saturday in late May he walked

---

Can you see the roofs above the clouds?
And if the mist rises
If the mist rises
The village will come
The village has come."
C. Lambert, *Tales from the Black Meadow* (Reading: Exiled Publications, 2013), p. 75.

with two friends onto the mist-shrouded moor. Like many artists of the current age he had dabbled in mysticism, he had experimented with herbs and medicines, tried to join obscure religious sects and had attempted to create music that went beyond the expectations of the everyday. He decided to seek out new experiences for himself. He had heard about the standing stones on the moors, as well as the great RAF Radomes[10] and the strange stories surrounding them.

As everybody knows, there are certain standing stones on the moors that require the visitor to take with them a sheet of parchment and some charcoal or wax crayon.[11] On locating the stone (after half a day of searching, he and his companions were not adept with an Ordnance Survey Map) he took a rubbing of a spiral that he found carved into the granite. His friends followed suit, before writing their worries and fears into the gaps between the spiral lines. The singer wrote in his concerns about his music, how he felt that he couldn't create what he envisioned. That task complete, they held the paper over a flame, watching their worries, concerns and hates disappearing into smoke and ash over the North York Moors.

---

[10] The Radomes at Fylingdales were three 40-metre-diameter 'golfballs' or geodesic domes (radomes) which, according to the RAF, contained mechanically steered radar. They were constructed in 1962 and demolished in the 1990s.
[11] There is a detailed reference made to this ritual in "The Standing Stone". C. Lambert, *Tales from the Black Meadow* (Reading: Exiled Publications, 2013), p. 41.

Mr Barrett and his three friends felt jubilant and free. They ran across the moors singing and dancing, stopping occasionally to look down strange holes or to roll in the heather. They made dens in the bramble. They ran into the mist trying to seek each other out by calls and chants.

In their delirious abandon, they found that they were drawing near to the RAF site on the North York Moors. Mr Barrett commented on the incongruity of the three spheres on the moors and encouraged his other two friends to see how close they could get to them. Not being tethered by the rules or mores of the establishment, they happily vaulted the high fences, making their way to the Radomes through a process of running, crouching and crawling. They were prepared to walk nonchalantly, as though lost, if met by officious soldiers. On this day, they were not accosted and came close to the first of the three Radomes. They flattened themselves against the base of the sphere, before peering around the side to check for any movement. Surrounding the sphere, furthest from them, were soldiers and a collection of men and women in long white coats. The soldiers were standing back whilst several of the scientists had their hands on the skin of the Radome. These scientists were standing still with their heads down. Mr Barrett assumed that they had their eyes closed. After a few minutes of stillness a scientist arched his back, falling into the arms of another scientist. A moment passed whilst the others flurried around, checking the scientist's pulse and waving smelling salts under his nose. The scientist spluttered, jumped to his feet and began to

231

pace and shout, gesticulating wildly. The others scribbled furious notes, listening carefully. The three travellers could hear snatches of words from where they watched. Cries of: "saw more... audire... father... vivid... audire..." A few minutes after he had finished his explanations, another scientist collapsed and a near identical process repeated: revival, shouting, gesticulation and notes.

Mr Barrett was very excited by what he had seen. He slowly stood and, while his friends watched, he placed his hands on the surface of the Radome. He commented on the light buzzing he could hear, the vibrations under his fingertips. Mr Barrett lowered his head, closed his eyes and listened.

The birds and sheep seemed louder somehow. More vibrant. Sounds were loud and fast, like the strange affliction he had suffered as a child in moments of isolation. When he was seven years old he suffering a prolonged illness, his hands seemed to expand inside, his skin became more sensitive and the voices of others grew acute and urgent, sounds had increased in volume, intensity and speed. He had forgotten all about that, but now it came back to him in a rush of images and feelings. He could hear his own heartbeat, the loud urgent breath of his two friends, he could hear the voices of the scientists.

"Just step through," one said. "I could just step through."

"I saw her," said another. "She was older, but I saw her."

"The dark and the fires," a third whispered. "All around. The dead air. The static. The fallen birds. The ruins."

232

He could hear another voice too.

"Have you got it yet?" It giggled. "Have you got it yet?"

The other voices, the sheep, the birds and the wind diminished into a static hiss.

"Have you got it yet?" The voice giggled again.

New sounds were heard. Cars outside. Children playing in the street. The slow ticking of a clock. The creaking of feet on floorboards. The skin of the Radome felt sticky, then soft. Mr Barrett pushed at it, allowing his arm to sink through the white custard membrane. He pushed his face through, opening his eyes to gaze upon the room he had heard. The room was empty of furniture and objects save for a guitar and a wooden chair. Upon the chair sat a large man with a shaved head staring at the guitar in the corner. He turned his head to look at Mr Barrett who had now stepped fully into the room.

"Oh it's you," he said. "I thought it would be."

Mr Barrett looked about the room again. He found it hard to speak.

"You don't need to speak," said the large bald man. "I didn't," he continued. "At least I don't think I did. My name's Roger."

Mr Barrett blinked, opening and shutting his mouth like a carp.

Roger got out of his chair, shuffling towards Mr Barrett. He peered at him through heavy set dark eyes. Mr Barrett stood stock still as Roger walked slowly around him.

"Have you got it yet?" he asked.

Mr Barrett found himself unable to speak. He was stiffening, his flesh crawling. He couldn't shake his head in response to the question.

233

"No you haven't," smiled Roger. "I didn't. Not until I woke up a few months ago."

Mr Barrett was finding it hard to breathe.

"Do you like what you see?"

The two of them stood staring at one another for an age. Mr Barrett could hear Roger's breathing, slow and deep. Could see the clammy sweat glinting on his face. Roger stepped away and walked towards the guitar.

"Do you play?"

Mr Barrett managed a nod at last.

"I don't think I do. I have been looking at it for some time, but I don't think I shall play it," Roger stated. "Will you?"

Roger picked up the guitar, strode over to Mr Barrett and passed him the instrument. Mr Barrett gasped at the feel of the wood in his hands, the delicate strings. He strummed a chord and began to play. Roger sank into his chair, slowly smiling. Mr Barrett played for several minutes and when he stopped, Roger took the guitar, thanking Mr Barrett gratefully for his efforts.

Roger walked back to Mr Barrett, who was standing stock still. Roger put his face close to Mr Barrett's.

"You will remember this," he whispered. "You will remember this, it will help for a while."

Roger reached out his hand to touch Mr Barrett's cheek.

"So young," he smiled. "Good times. Good times. I wish I was there."

As Roger's finger brushed against Mr Barrett's skin there was a surge of green light. The sounds of cars, children playing and the soft creak of footsteps on floorboards was replaced by the cries of birds, sheep, a soft breeze and the distant murmurings of scientists.

He fell. The room was gone, in its place was the vast sphere filling every part of his vision. His two friends helped him to his feet. They carefully made their way back to the fence, unnoticed by the groups of scientists and soldiers immersed in their work.

Inside *The Plough* Inn, Mr Barrett was taciturn. He drunk his one pint of ale and wandered off to his bed with barely a word, lost in thought. In the morning his friends were relieved to see him laughing and joking with the landlady, whilst he scoffed down one of her delicious cooked breakfasts. His friends pressed him to tell them again what he had seen but he told them it was all a blur. In fact anything he did see was probably his imagination anyway.

Mr Barrett drove to Lincolnshire that day to play an incredible set with his new band and for a while everything was wonderful.

20th Century Encounters

The Wretched Stranger

The Wretched Stranger

It was his eyes. His eyes were the first thing she noticed. One sat on the branch of a tree, the red root dangling down, whilst the other was skewered on bramble thorns. His head lay on the ground just in front of the tree, mouth open and closing, teeth bloody, tongue lolling. His limbs were thrown hither and yon. His torso sat nonchalantly against the tree. The mouth was still opening and closing. She leaned in close, bloodied fingers gripping the shaft of the axe tightly. The bloodied lips tried to form words but there was no breath to create volume. She stepped closer still, bending her ear to the bloody mouth.

"I cannot see," it whispered. "What has happened? Is that you Camilla?"

Camilla, for she it was, stiffened.

The mouth whispered again, "Let me see it..."

Camilla raised the axe and brought the blade crashing down, deep into the bone of the head on the ground. She brought it down again and again until the whispering ceased.

*   *   *

The stranger lifted his bowler hat to scratch his head.

"Do you not know where you are?"

The stranger shook his head and smiled benignly.

Tom Fullerton the Postmaster gazed at the strange man in black suit and tie. Jet black hair

241

beneath pristine hat, perfect unblemished skin and no trace of a beard or stubble. Skin like a baby.

"I confess," said the stranger in a stilted and faltering tone. "That I am lost."

"Where were you heading?"

"I do not know."

"Have you hurt your head?"

"I do not think so."

"What's your name?"

"I do not know. Do I need a name?"

"Most people do. Certainly in my line of work. Otherwise who would you send the letters to?"

An automobile roared past the window. The stranger jumped and gave a high pitched yelp of fright.

"What was that?"

Tom stared at the stranger.

"That was a van."

"Why is it so loud?"

"Was it? I don't know. Might be that Enoch's still got an issue with his engine."

"Who is Enoch?"

"Enoch is the Greengrocer. He drives the van. Making deliveries."

"Enoch has an engine?"

"Er, yes."

"That is good. I must speak to him."

Tom studied the stranger closely. His eyes were dull, no moisture or light reflected from them. As he stared at the gentleman he felt a wave of emotion sweep over him. He shuddered. He wanted to strike this man but he could not fathom why. He had done nothing to harm him. No word of offence had passed his lips. And yet. If he reached across now he could

242

grab him by the collar with both hands and smash his skull with his own. He blinked, the man was speaking.

"Thank you. You have been most helpful."

Inexplicably he found himself speaking through gritted teeth.

"Are you sure you don't need any further assistance, sir? You seem lost."

"Lost?" The stranger nodded. "I am lost. That is good."

The stranger held out his hand. Tom went to grasp it, fearing that if that strange perfect skin touched his that he would be unable to control himself. He would snap. The cold dry hand closed over his.

"Thank you," said the stranger.

The letter opener was in Tom's other hand. He wasn't sure how long he had been holding it. But he was aware of it now, sweeping up in a wide arc, round and down into the chest of this perfectly pleasant gentleman. The stranger released his grip of Tom's hand before looking down at his chest, blood pooling around the handle of the blade.

"Oh," he said. "Should that be there?"

Tom blinked and shook his head to clear the haze. What had he done? He had cleansed the world of this wretched stranger. A perfect hit. And yet. The man still stood looking at him.

"Is this a gift?"

The stranger's hand moved up and grasped the handle of the letter opener. As he pulled it from his chest, warm scarlet splattered onto Tom's face and into his gaping mouth. It tasted sweet.

"Thank you," said the stranger.

243

Tom gawped. The stranger looked concerned.

"But I have nothing for you. Wait a moment."

The stranger opened his briefcase, reaching inside.

"Would you like a pencil?"

Tom could not speak. His confusion at what the man was doing, coupled with his unfounded hatred for him, left his mouth opening and shutting like a landed fish.

"So, how does this work?" The stranger smiled gently, bringing his arm round in a wide arc, sweeping up and down until the pencil was sticking out of Tom's chest. Tom staggered back. His knees buckled. Bubbles of blood formed instead of a scream. The stranger wiped the letter opener, put it inside the briefcase and turned to leave. He doffed his cap to Tom, now sitting slumped on the floor.

"Thank you so much," he said. "You have been very kind."

The bell on the door sang out as the stranger stepped onto the street. Tom gurgled before falling onto his side.

*   *   *

"What have you done to yourself?" said Enoch, wiping his hands on an oily rag and pointing at the Stranger's bloody chest.

"What have I done?" The stranger looked down. "Oh that. Do not worry. It's not real."

"Oh right. What can I do you for?"

"I want to see your engine."

"Which one?"

244

"The Postmaster told me you were having trouble with your engine. I would like to see it."

"You a mechanic?"

"Of a sort."

"You don't look like a mechanic."

The stranger cocked his head to one side and smiled.

"There's nothing much going on with it," Enoch said. "Just the usual."

"What is the usual?"

"You know, the pipes are a bit clogged. Probably needs some oil running through it. Bit of a clean out. I'll have to take it apart."

"You can take your own engine apart?"

Enoch stared at the stranger. There was something not right about him. As well as the drying deep scarlet circle decorating the front of his shirt, the smooth unblemished perfect skin and his uncanny smile, there was something about him that Enoch disliked intensely. He backed to his toolbox. His hand searched and rooted about until it found the wrench.

"Where'd you come from? You from the town?"

"I am not from the town."

"How did you get here?

"I walked. Can I help you with your engine?"

"Of course. Come and take a look."

Enoch stepped aside, allowing the stranger to see the raised bonnet of his van. However, the stranger moved towards Enoch himself. He stood close to him, placing his briefcase down upon the workbench.

"Thank you. You are very kind."

The stranger opened the briefcase. He reached inside. There was a click. A low hum. From the yawning mouth of the briefcase flowed a snaking blanket of mist. It drifted to the floor and began to fill every corner of the room.

"Breathe in, Mr Enoch," the stranger ordered.

Enoch could not fight the overwhelming desire to strike this man. He felt a hatred for this stranger that he had never experienced before. This perfect, bland gentleman. His hand gripped the wrench harder. The mist reached his nostrils.

"Let me take a look at your engine."

The stranger leant in. In his hand was a shining metal stick. He drew it up and pointed one end at the centre of Enoch's forehead. From the end of the stick, thin threads of silver sprouted out, splitting and snaking around Enoch's skull until they joined to form a ring. The ring began to shrink until the thread was tight and biting into Enoch's skin.

"Breathe in, Mr Enoch," the stranger ordered.

Blood started to pool over the thread as it cut a red line around his skull. Enoch screamed in pain and rage. He flung his arm around, smashing the wrench against this wretched stranger's skull. The stranger reeled to the side. His perfect fingers released the spike and the threads loosened allowing Enoch to extricate himself from the tight grip of the wire.

The stranger staggered for a moment before standing upright. His head was dented by the blow from the wrench, the skin broken and torn. Blood pooled in the cracks.

"I want to help," he said.

Enoch walked over to the stranger and raised his wrench again. He brought it crashing down upon the other side of his head. There was a gasp at the door. Enoch turned to face Camilla. She stared, open-mouthed at Enoch. The upper quarter of his head was oozing blood from a perfect horizontal line onto his face. A bloodied wrench dangled from his hand. It clattered to the floor. Enoch swayed, Camilla ran forward to steady him.

"Father!"

"He did this, Camilla."

Camilla guided Enoch to a chair. She found a scarf to wrap tight around his head before wiping his dark scarlet face clean with a cloth.

There was a low whispering rasp. Camilla turned her head. The stranger stood, staring at the scene.

"I want to help," he said. "If you will allow me I would like to examine his engine. The Postmaster said there was something wrong with it."

Camilla glared at the stranger.

"We do not need your help, once father is well enough to stand I shall take him to the doctor and call the constabulary."

"Oh. I should like to meet them," smiled the stranger. His smile was oddly emphasised by the large concave dents at his temples coupled with his apparent nonchalance towards the injuries he had sustained.

Camilla helped her father to his feet. As they reached the door she turned to the stranger.

"Be warned. Although my priority is my father, if you evade the police I will find you myself. I am stronger than I look."

"Aye," nodded Enoch, wincing. "She is at that."

247

"I shall go and meet the constabulary now. If that will be of assistance," the stranger grinned doffing his hat.

Camilla and Enoch left the garage. The stranger placed the stick inside his briefcase, fastening the clasp before carrying it to the door.

*   *   *

When Camilla got to the police station she was surprised to find it silent. Papers werc strewn across the floor. A desk was upended and the cell door was open. Lying on the floor, half in and half out of the cell, was Constable Staverton. He was groaning. His legs were splayed, his head turned to one side and his feet sat on the desk, several yards from the rest of him.

Camilla searched about to find something to bind the stumps of his legs, to stop the blood flowing anymore. She pulled off her belt to fix the right foot and used the telephone cord for the left.

"What happened?"

Constable Staverton groaned. "Stranger came."

"What did he do?"

"He seemed so nice. But I couldn't help but take a dislike to him. I was dealing with Harry –you know Harry."

"I know Harry."

Everyone knew Harry.

"He'd had one too many, and he was his normal self. Swearing up a blue storm. But when he called me flatfoot…"

Constable Staverton sobbed for a minute. Camilla wiped his face with a tissue from the desk.

"The stranger seemed to get really interested. He asked if he could see them. He opened his briefcase and there was this light. My feet. Where are my feet?"

"They're on the desk."

The constable tried to sit up. Camilla shushed him, laying a hand on his shoulder.

"Don't try to move."

"Is Harry still here?"

"I think he's gone."

"Typical."

"I'll call the ambulance."

Constable Staverton stifled another sob. "Thank you, Camilla. You've got a heart of gold you have."

"Just lie still."

Camilla stood up. She turned to the phone. The stranger was standing behind the desk. He was smiling. "A heart of gold?" He grinned. "That sounds very interesting. Can I see?"

The stranger opened his briefcase. Camilla ran for the door.

The stranger followed with a jaunty step. Camilla could hear him behind her. Even though she was running, he appeared to be keeping pace, even with his own slow measured walk. She ran, her breath coming out in frightened gasps. He walked, a smile on his mouth. And no matter how fast she ran, no matter what twists and turns she took, he was always ten paces behind her.

Camilla had made it to the garage. She ran inside, locking the door quickly behind her. The axe was by the workbench. She lifted it up, feeling the weight of it, giving a few experimental swings. The metal door rattled. A sharp bright pinprick of light was glowing at the lock. Smoke and sparks issued from the metal. She scrambled for the door to the kitchen, locking it behind her.

She was out of the front door within seconds. He had heard her and was strolling around the side of the garage. She ran. He walked. She gasped. He smiled. Ten paces behind.

The wheat field was just ahead. The combine harvester slowly making its way along the hedge-line. She sprinted for it. Darting through the hedge. Slowing and waiting as the combine rattled closer. Ensuring that the driver did not see her until the last minute. Allowing the wretched stranger to catch up. She could hear him cracking at branches, making his way closer and closer. The blades of the combine were feet away now, turning with their mechanical viciousness. A hand grabbed at her shoulder. She pulled away, sprinting along the line of blades, feeling the harsh breeze of their movement. He was three paces behind.

There was no noise as the combine harvester struck the stranger.

It rattled on, leaving a trail of scarlet and scattered limbs behind.

Camilla looked at the carnage and smiled.

*   *   *

When she had finished hacking at his skull with her axe, she ran back to the police station. Constable Staverton was still conscious. She called for the ambulance, accompanying the constable on his journey as her father would be at the hospital too.

When the authorities visited the scene the remains of the stranger were gone, but there was a lot of blood.

The briefcase was resting by the hedge. It was pristine and unharmed. Try as they might they could not open it, not by picking the lock or by cutting the leather. They decided that although it had the appearance of leather that this was not a material they had encountered before. Even Grandpa Jack, the last of the Tanner line, could not make head nor tail of it.

The briefcase was locked away in the evidence room at the police station. A few weeks later the police constable in charge of the evidence room reported that a man from the ministry had collected it. This man had shown all the correct papers and so the constable had handed it over. He did recall that this gentleman was rather bland in appearance with a bowler hat on his head and that he couldn't help but take an instant dislike to him. But then, he put that down to the fact that the man clearly worked for the government.

20th Century Encounters

The Village Under the Lake

The Village Under the Lake

The body lay on the shore of Gormire. Face-up, arms by its side, pale skin with blotches of blue and purple around the mouth and cheeks. Eyes open. On this cold March morning flies had yet to discover this morsel and it was clear that it had not lain there for long. Black hair was caked around the sides of the head framing the face.

Constable Jones' eyes shifted from the face of the corpse to that of his superior who was staring down in disbelief.

"Identification?" The doctor was kneeling next to the shoulders of the corpse.

"We didn't find any," said Constable Jones. "Though at first we thought it was..."

Detective Winstanley cleared his throat. "Can you determine the cause of death sir?"

"Too early to say," the doctor staggered to his feet. "There are no signs of struggle. No cuts. No bruises." He swept his arm across the view of the lake. "I would suggest drowning."

"The victim, he..."

"Yes he does, doesn't he, detective. He's the spitting image in fact."

"How is that possible?"

"Do you have a brother?"

"No."

"A cousin?"

"Well... yes, but..."

"This can happen. Every so often we hear about people bumping into their doubles. No relation but for some reason they are the same build, same hair colour and facial features. It is an accident of birth, the hereditary features mould from generation to generation and for some reason one can mirror another from a distinct and separate line. Call it coincidence."

"It's rather unsettling."

"It is, isn't it? If I was in your shoes I'd be rocking back and forth in a corner right now, crossing myself and praying to God and all his angels."

"The key thing then is not to allow this to distract us."

The constable cleared his throat.

"I've taken his prints sir, so if he has committed a crime... I can look through the files and see if there's a match. And I've also put out a call to see if anyone – ahem – matches his description."

Detective Winstanley lit a cigarette and inhaled deeply. "Look through *Missing Persons* as well."

"Of course, sir."

There was a yell of surprise. They turned their heads. One of the constables was pointing out towards the lake. They followed his finger. Bobbing in the water, face up, was the figure of a man.

"Good god," whispered the doctor.

The police constable waded into the water to pull the body to shore. The three men ran forward as the burly constable carried the figure out of the water before laying it at their feet. The doctor knelt down to brush the hair from the face of the corpse. As his hand moved across its face he jumped up as though stung. His eyes darted up to Constable Jones who looked down in alarm.

"A second coincidence?"

"That is very unlikely indeed."

Constable Jones simply stood mute, staring at the body that shared his own face.

The Doctor regained his composure, gingerly lowering himself to his knees with a series of cracks and pops. He went through the motions of checking, his previous reaction forgotten. Constable Jones went to speak but the flurry of activity on the ground stopped him. The Doctor was bent over the chest of the body, shoulders stiff, hands clasped, pushing down five times in rhythm, before stopping and breathing twice into the mouth. He repeated this sequence several times until suddenly the body, with Constable Jones' face, sat up and vomited a stream of water. He sat there, blinking wildly for a moment before sitting unsteadily.

"Back..." said the resurrected man who looked like Constable Jones. The trio duly stepped back. The Jones doppelganger jumped to his feet, looked left and right as if getting its bearings, before running for the path to the road. Winstanley glanced at the others, beckoning them to follow.

When they approached the road they could see Constable Jones' motorcycle speeding off around a corner. The Doctor and Jones bundled into Winstanley's car without a word. Winstanley jumped into the driver's seat. The car coughed and spluttered, rumbling down the road, its hard rubber tyres crackling against the earth track.

The tiny motorcycle pootled ahead in the distance – twisting and turning on the tiny pale grey spaghetti lanes that worked their way up towards the moors.

"Good god," gasped the doctor. "He must be doing close to forty miles an hour. Did you know your bike could do that Jones?"

Jones was tight-lipped, his eyes slightly glazed.

"This fellow can barely get above thirty five," snarled Winstanley, his foot down hard in the well. The car rocked back and forth, knocking its three occupants to its four corners as the driver attempted to master the turns of the track.

The motorcycle disappeared over the brow of the hill. After a minute or so they found themselves at that very same point but looking out into a vast grey fog.

"Blast," growled Winstanley, switching on the headlamps which simply highlighted the density of the fog rather than penetrating it in any way. The car slowed to a careful crawl. It was almost impossible to see more than a few feet ahead.

"We'll never catch him now," moaned the doctor.

Constable Jones stared out of the window.

"Stop the car," he ordered.

The car shuddered to a halt. Jones leapt out, without stopping to close his door, and ran to the heather. The other two swiftly followed. There, lying in the verge, was the motorcycle. Jones touched the engine, withdrawing his hand with a wince.

"He's only just left," he said.

The three peered out into the fog.

"Which way did the fellow go?" the doctor asked.

"Into the mist," said Winstanley.

Winstanley instructed the Doctor to stay by the car whilst he and Jones ventured into the fog to look for the missing doppelganger. Doctor Trent followed their exit from the safety of the car. He lost sight of them after about half a minute but could hear them calling out for the stranger for some time after. But even those strident yells soon faded away. He sat to wait for their return. At noon the mist swiftly faded and Trent looked out across the vast and empty moor. He though he saw a glimpse of smoke from a chimney but it vanished as the mist faded to nothing. Of the detective and the constable there was no sign. He got out of the car and called for them for a while, but on hearing no reply he decided to drive on to the station to seek help.

The body was laid out on a metal table in the back room, eyes closed, stripped of clothing. The doctor rushed in without a glance. The inspector glanced up from his paperwork.

"Where's Jones and Winstanley?"

"I don't know. You need to get out there on the moor. We followed the thief – the man from Gormire Lake – the one who looked like..."

"Jones?"

"We followed him but lost him in the mist. We stopped when we found the motorcycle. They got out to search for him. I waited for an hour. The mist cleared. They were nowhere."

The inspector asked Doctor Trent to explain exactly where they had gone missing. He called three constables and ordered them into a van. As he was about to leave he turned to the doctor.

"The body is ready for you. We took the fingerprints – the results are... well. Take a look for yourself." He went to leave but stopped again. "Oh, and there's an old gentleman at the front desk waiting to see you."

"To see me?"

"I said he'd need to wait. He said that wouldn't be a problem."

Doctor Trent called the surgery to cancel his practice appointments for the rest of the day asking if his partner could see the most urgent patients. He pulled back the sheet and studied the body of Winstanley's lookalike. There was a ragged scar on his arm. He bent closer to take a look. He had... no it couldn't be. Catching himself mumbling in consternation he wandered over to the book. The incident report was tatty and well thumbed.

"February last year," he mumbled. "February 1949."

He peered and muttered as he found the right page, examining the information recorded in his own almost indecipherable scrawl.

Inspector Cavendish had banged his head on a bookshelf in his office.

"No."

Constable Jones – bruise to right cheek breaking up altercation at The Plough.

"That was it."

The next one read: *Detective Winstanley deep cut to upper right arm by broken bottle sustained breaking up altercation at The Plough.*

"I sutured that bugger myself. Yes."

Trent ran over to the front desk.

"The folder?"

"What folder?" Constable Fortune asked.

"Fingerprints of John Doe?"

"What, Winstanley Two?"

"That's not funny, Fortune."

262

"No sir. Sorry sir." He passed a file over to the doctor. "There's a man here to see you."

Fortune pointed at an old gentleman sitting on a leather sofa under the window. The old man started to rise, Trent glanced at him, grabbed the folder from Fortune's hand before returning to the back room. The old man slowly lowered himself back into his seat.

Trent's eyes darted from the corpse's fingerprints to the identical comparison pulled from the files. There was no mistake. The name on the file spelled it out in no uncertain terms: Winstanley, James.

He ran to the front desk waving the folder in Fortune's face.

"Is this a joke? Because there just isn't the time."

"No joke sir."

"Then what is going on?"

"I might be able to help," stated a voice from the waiting area. Both turned their eyes to the old man sitting under the window. Fortune leaned forward over the desk. "It's old Eddy from the farm, isn't it?"

"That's right," said the old man. "In a way."

"How can you help? You've run your blackberry and dairy farm for what, 50 years?"

"Closer to sixty now, young fella."

"Sixty years. Blackberry and dairy. Blackberry and dairy. Nothing else. See you at market at end of season. What would you know about anything other than blackberries and pints of bloody milk?"

"I've been waiting."

"Yeah, well. I'm sorry about that, Eddy, but we do have other things to worry about other than your needs. What you do? Lose a bramble?"

"I need to speak to the doctor."

263

Trent looked up from his continued scrutiny of the fingerprints, "Can it wait?"

"Not any longer."

"All right. But it will have to be quick."

Doctor Trent walked into the waiting area. Eddy stood. He took off his cap, wisps of white, almost transparent hair dancing free.

"Look at me."

"What?"

"Come into the light. Look at me in the light."

Doctor Trent shrugged and moved forward, scrutinising the old man as requested.

"Do I know you?"

"Not well. But you have tended to me on more than one occasion."

"You're not on my books, sir. Are you sure?"

"I was on your books."

"When?"

"A good few years ago."

"When I was in Pickering? I don't recall."

"No it was here."

Trent shook his head. He was beginning to realise that this old man must be somewhat confused.

"I'm so sorry, sir," he started, "But if you'd like to make an appointment at the surgery, I can..."

The old man smiled and shook his head. Without a word he brushed past Doctor Trent, walked around the desk, past an astonished Constable Fortune and into the back room. Fortune and Trent looked after the old man, looked at each other, before swiftly following him.

When they entered the room, they found Eddy at a table with an ink stamp blacking the fingers of his right hand before making a mark on a sheet of paper. He wiped his hand on the sheet covering the other Winstanley.

"Sir?" Constable Fortune said, "I need to get back to the front desk."

The doctor nodded. Eddy walked over to Trent, he pointed to the folder in his hands.

"Is that Personnel? It should be in there."

"What should be in there?"

Eddy pulled the folder from Trent's grasp. Before he could take it back, Eddy was flipping through the file with the deft movements of someone who knew exactly where to look. The old man pulled out the file belonging to Constable Jones.

"Constable Edward Jones. I remember the day these were taken."

"Are you related to him? Do you know where he is?"

"I do. I know exactly where he is."

He held up the still wet fingerprints and placed them next to the smudges on file. Trent's eyes moved from one set to the other.

"That's not possible."

"And yet it is."

"Are you his grandfather?"

"Fingerprints don't work that way. Look at me."

"I am."

"And?"

"It isn't possible. You can't…"

"And yet I am."

Doctor Trent stepped closer. He raised his hands to the old man's face.

"May I?"

The old man nodded. Trent proceeded to prod and pull the skin. He checked his heart rhythm, breathing, ears, reflexes, teeth and eyes. He sat down, his wide eyes still scanning Eddy's features.

"I can see a resemblance between you and Constable Jones. Your fingerprints match, aside from some general wear and tear on your own fingers. I am at a loss."

Eddy smiled. "Then let me explain," he said. "I have waited nearly sixty years for this day."

Doctor Trent leant against the table bearing the corpse of Detective Winstanley. Old Eddy sat down in a stout wooden chair by the filing cabinet.

"Good man, Winstanley," he said, gesturing to the body. "Kind to me he was. I didn't think twice about following him into the mist. That said, I was fascinated to discover just who the fellow was we were chasing. We left you at the car, what, about two hours ago?"

Trent nodded, tight-lipped. Every ounce of his being fighting the urge to blurt out "This is nonsense," before storming from the room. There had to be some explanation. He listened.

"Well, we couldn't see a thing in front of us and so we walked, in what we assumed was a straight line, for over an hour. The ground barely changed underfoot, we had to avoid lumps and patches of bog here and there, but it was formless and we couldn't see a sign of my double anywhere. Our calls had gone unanswered. The going got rougher, at times it seemed as though the ground itself moved beneath our feet. We saw the grass and heather shrink from full seeded blade and flower to stalk, to sprig, to seed, to dried and dead shrub, to vibrant purple, to green shoot, to bare ground, over and over. The terrain changed. We had to walk around shrinking bushes, pass through a small wood with brown leaves flying up to bare branches before turning to green leaves and buds. The ground began to incline downwards sharply. The mist cleared, leaving a dense cloud above our heads. We found ourselves on the side of a steep valley and far below us we could see a small village at the very bottom. Winstanley and I hadn't spoken a word but at this point he admitted to me that he was totally lost. I did not recognise the place either. He suggested we make enquiries at this village to, at the very least, get our bearings.

The village was alive with sound and music. In the centre a broken down and ruined church was the centrepiece of a joyous celebration. There were a group of men dancing with sheep skulls for hats and a decorated thigh bone, with a bell jingling on the end, in each hand. A group of women were drinking drafts of ale from deep wooden bowls. The eldest children sat reading under trees or stirring enormous pots of stew over several fires, whilst the smallest served the stew on large plates to the assembled throng.

It was Winstanley who approached them first. I could tell he was bewildered by it all, he took a great gulp of air before waving his hat and yelling out a "Hallo!"

The dancers froze, their bones hanging limp in their hands, the bells slowly jingling to a stop. The children serving stew hid behind the skirts of their inebriated mothers, whilst the various cooks stilled their wooden spoons. All eyes were on Winstanley.

"Hallo," he tried again. "We are looking for a man. He looks like..."

He gestured me forward. The dancers gathered about me, their sheep skulls waggling dangerously before my face. A woman rose from the table, she was old and wide with skin as green as meadow grass. The others sported skin of different hues, pinks, blues and hideous pale whites. Their eyes all sparkled emerald as they looked upon us. The sheep skulls parted to let her through. The woman, the elder, as I thought she was, approached Winstanley, a flagon of ale in her hand. She mumbled a phrase.

"I'm sorry," Winstanley said. "I didn't quite catch that."

The woman laughed, grabbing his face between the fingers of her fat right hand, grinning and howling into his face. Winstanley tried to move his head but she held it fast. He flailed his arms, bringing them around to prise her fingers free from his face. She raised the flagon high and tipped it so the ale poured free over his face and into his open mouth. Winstanley sputtered and choked; the green woman laughed. The villagers, surrounding me in their bright blue bonnets and leather caps, clapped and cheered.

Winstanley looked over at me. I remember that expression so vividly. How those eyes, so wide with terror, pricked with frightened tears changed to a dull and peaceful daydream. How that mouth, flecked with spittle and beer became a wide beatific smile. His body loosened, his hands relaxed. The green woman stepped back and offered him the flagon of ale. Winstanley's hands reached out eagerly. The rim of the jug kissed his lips and the ale poured into his mouth. The crowd cheered, raising their arms into the air, clapping their hands wildly. The cheer turned into a chant. Words unintelligible, vowel sounds repeated over and over, running into each other. Winstanley's eyes were glazed as his gaze briefly found mine. I tried to edge forward, but the people around me placed hands on my chest and back. Others gripped my shoulders. Winstanley turned and walked towards the church. The crowd parted, allowing him through. He strode with an unsteady yet certain step through the rotten lych gate, between the tottering gravestones before stepping through the yawning doorway. As he stepped into the darkness beyond, the crowd moved forward. They became quiet. The chant diminishing to a whisper before petering away to mutterings, mummery, breath and silence. I found myself propelled forward with them. The blue and pink and yellow and purple and red faces stared straight ahead – there was no acknowledgement of my struggles or my cries as I was pushed and pulled into the interior of the church. The nave was lit by sunlight through shattered glass. The remnants of a half Christ casting his broken blessings upon this cursed population.

The green painted woman stood at what was the altar but now was dominated by an enormous eye constructed from different coloured grasses and flowers. In the centre of the church below the pulpit was a pool of pitch black water. Piles of stone slabs adorned the sides, removed to allow access to the soil beneath, the results of that excavation sat at the foot of the pulpit. The earth stretched up to the rim of the pulpit, indicating that the pool was quite deep. A group of twelve brightly coloured people moved to the edge of the pool, lowering themselves into the

269

dark fluid until they stood in two rows of six on either side, creating an aisle for someone to walk through. That someone was Winstanley.

He was standing at the edge of the pool, swaying slightly, looking directly at the green-skinned woman who stood directly in front of the iris of the giant eye. The silence ended as the green skinned woman let out an elongated yodel. This was joined by the rest, firstly as a low hum, before building to a chant full of an impossible mix of vowels and consonants. Winstanley moved forward, his body swaying in time to the sounds of the crowd. The twelve in the pool lifted their hands from the murky depths, the blues and pinks and yellows streaking away to reveal dark green palms and fingers waving in the dusty air.

The green skinned woman threw her head back, opening her mouth, a gargling call erupting from within. Winstanley stood close to the centre of the pool. The twelve lowered their hands on to his shoulders, head and arms. The sound continued building as each of the twelve joined with various pitches and tones. Winstanley slowly sunk to his knees so that the level of the water came up to his chin. The hands pressed down. His head lowered beneath the surface. I was struggling hard against these strange villagers. Bubbles popped and glooped up through the murk of the pool. The green-skinned woman walked to the edge. I glanced around at the gathered bizarre congregation realising that all were sporting green skin beneath their brightly coloured exteriors. At her feet was an iron rod running through the centre of the first link in an iron chain, the bulk of which disappeared into the murk. She bent down, taking one side of the rod in each of her hands. She sang out a long high note that was joined by the others in a strangely beautiful cacophony. She stood up straight, pulling the chain out of the water. The water churned and swirled. The twelve removed their hands from the hidden Winstanley, bringing them out of the water to clamp together, holding themselves steady as the water level dropped violently. As the water level lowered, droplets of clear water began to drip down from above the pool. Looking up they came not from a hole in the roof as expected but appeared from a spot in the air some ten feet above the swirling water. The droplets increased in number, becoming a mist of rain, a shower, until they ran, like a cascade of water over a cliff-side. The roar was immense. The screaming chant of the crowd was now barely audible above the cacophony. They were all looking up at this strange phenomenon. I felt the grip on my shoulders lessen. Quickly I broke free, sprinting for the pool. I ran in, flailing my arms, searching for Winstanley, the waterfall smashing at my head, but the space where he must have been was now a whirling sucking void. I took a deep breath, ducked under, opening my eyes to see nothing but black, brackish brown. My feet slipped on the slimy clay beneath me and I found myself plunging to the centre. Unable to fight the current I held my breath, finding myself spinning downwards into the dark, deeper and deeper, then sideways for a length – I thought I could see a body ahead of me rising up towards the light. As I was pulled to the same point I too rose and for a while I blacked out.

271

Doctor Trent stared at the old man.

"I can barely understand this."

"Neither could I," The old man continued. "And yet when I woke and saw Winstanley's corpse I felt nothing but a burning desire for justice. And even in my bewildered state I understood that no-one would believe my story, and, even if they did, too much time would be lost. So I fought to ignore my own reflection looking back at me from only hours before. I blocked out the very much alive Winstanley standing above his own corpse, leapt to my feet, found my motorcycle and drove back in a desperate attempt to retrace my steps.

I found the strange wall of mist and left the motorbike. I realised after some time walking back that on the first journey we were so turned about and befuddled by the mist that we had simply come full circle. That the site of this village I described before was the same site as Gormire itself. Gormire as it is now is a deep lake, but we had gone to Gormire then...sometime in the distant past or on some other level of existence. I did not know. But now there is a strange clarity to my thoughts. I have had time to consider this. The whirlpool of water had spat me out to an earlier point. I might be able to get to the village before Winstanley and put a stop to their wickedness. If that was impossible then these villains would not escape censure. I would put an end to their wicked ways. But the mist I walked through was deeper than before. It felt cooler on my still sodden clothes. I could feel the ground shifting beneath my feet again. Grass growing from shoot to full seeded blade in patterns of high speed over and over until I emerged blinking, looking out over that same village I had left not an hour before.

I ran down the hill, tumbling and weaving through the heather, finally coming to a stop in the centre. I looked about me. A green-skinned child was standing by the door of her house. She screamed as she saw me and ran inside, slamming her door shut. A few green heads peered out at windows, ducking out of sight when I glanced their way. All of my attention was on the church ahead. It looked in a worse state of repair than before. The walls of the porch were daubed with strange images of pools swirling, green-skinned figures with mouths open, screaming and fleeing from a striking image in the centre. That figure in the centre was of a pale skinned man with dripping skin and hair, a roaring grimace, razor sharp teeth, burning red eyes and arms in the sir. In his hands were two halves of a giant woven eye, torn asunder. Above this figure was painted an immense pool of water that spread along the length of the wall, up onto the ceiling over my head, to the other side of the porch. I ran my fingers though my still wet hair. A gasp to my left. Standing just inside the church, her back to the pool and tattered altar beyond was the green-skinned woman. Her eyes wide and her mouth caught in a terrified gape. Her hair was a shock of white with a few flecks of green. Her emerald eyes were dull and bloodshot. Her green skin wrinkled and dry. She backed towards the pool.

"I have returned," I shouted.

She staggered backwards, lost her footing and plunged into the dark brown pool. I ran to the other side to pull up the chain. She had found her way to her feet and let out a great cry as she saw me yank at the chain. A crowd of people had gathered at the door and they let out a collective low moan as their priestess sank into the vortex. The water poured from above and although the pool continued to swirl, the volume was far greater and the liquid in the pool was soon lapping at the edges before spilling out over into the church. The people screamed and shook, holding onto each other as they saw their unholy temple fill, the water pouring down the aisle towards them. I ran to the altar, lifting the grass eye above my head, bending and tearing at its structure until two halves sat in my hands. I shouted my curse at the green-skins in the porch, glaring at them through the cascading falls. The water lapped at the ancient stone altar, it poured out the doors, rising and rising. The whirlpool appeared now as an inconsequential eddy, apparently vague and harmless in the rising waters. However as the water rose and I could find no higher ground I could feel its immense pull and was swept towards the centre. Down, down, down, then sideways for a while. As my lungs began to burn I thought I could see the old woman drifting ahead of me, her green body limp, but she disappeared, pulled by another current. Above me I could see other bodies, some in frantic movement, others still moving downwards and round. My lungs gave out, I took in a deep breath and found myself rising towards the light as my lungs filled with water."

Doctor Trent wiped his hand across his forehead, nervously reaching for a cigarette.

"But how did you... why are you... as you are now?"

"I awoke once again on the shore of the lake. I was spitting water from my mouth and an old man was sitting by my side. He was panting with effort as he had taken some time to revive me. After I sat up he walked me away from the lake to his cart. We rode on the track to where the station is now, but there were just a few buildings, the pub, the church and a couple of houses. Very different from what I knew. Like the old photographs in the village hall. I turned to the old man, Farmer Talchester was his name, and he could tell me nothing of a police station and he had no idea who I was. He did tell me that there was a young man called Winstanley whose wife was expecting a baby. I was told that he was a good man. This farmer gave me board. He was a lonely old man and happy for my help and company who looked upon me as a son of sorts. When he died, having no family of his own he left the farm to me. I searched for the village, I could find the lake of course but the village eluded me and the mist never led me back there. So I farmed and so I waited. I waited for you. I waited to be able to pay my respects to him."

Trent and Eddie Jones looked across at the corpse on the table.

After a while Trent turned to the old man. "What will you do now?"

The door slammed open and Constable Fortune stood staring at them.

"What is it?"

"It's the lake sir," Fortune stammered. "I just got a call, sir. There's more bodies. Dozens sir. And they're..."

Doctor Trent looked at the aged Constable Jones, "Green?"

"That's right. How did…"

Fortune stopped speaking. He was staring at a man standing behind the table. He was wearing a sharp pin stripe suit, wearing a black bowler hat and carrying a dark briefcase. He had not been standing there when Fortune had entered the room. At least Fortune didn't think so.

"I am from the ministry," said the man in a calm and quiet tone. "There's nothing to worry about. We'll take it from here."

Two more men entered the room, pushing Constable Fortune out of the way. They placed Winstanley into a black body bag as the three men watched in astonished silence, before carrying him from the building.

"Now look here," said Trent, rising to his feet.

The bowler-hatted man put his finger to his lips and opened his briefcase.

And Doctor Trent, Constable Fortune and Eddie Jones did not speak of this incident again.

20th Century Encounters

Ghost Planes

Ghost Planes

What follows is a fictionalised account of events recounted in an interview Roger Mullins gave in 1968. This is coupled with a selection of notes by Roger Mullins under the title "Ghost Planes and Land Shadows".

As Roger Mullins waited in *The Plough* at Sleights he gazed out of the window at the blue sky. It was empty of clouds and birds. A half-sipped pint of warm ale sat at his elbow. Turning, he knocked it slightly, causing the glass to spill over one of the documents sitting on the table in front of him. He uttered a Maori curse which caused a couple of punters to look up in alarm.

The landlord called over to his table. "You all right, Mr Mullins?"

"Oh god," Roger said in his slightly panicky Christchurch brogue. "I am ever so sorry."

"S'alright," the landlord grinned. "No bloody idea what you said anyway. Was that your Indian language?"

"Maori, Mr Quickly," Roger corrected him. "Picked up a few bad habits when I spent a couple of years on the North Island."

Roger wiped the map dry with the sleeve of his tweed jacket. His eyes scanned the table. The map in the centre was surrounded by photographs, snatches of writings, old manuscripts, torn notes, sketches and diagrams. A circle was drawn around a key point on the map. In the middle of the circle was printed the word: "Fylingdales."

Roger took a hearty swig from his glass. The landlord called over from the bar. "What you lookin' at there, Mr Mullins?"

"Stories, evidence, folklore. Probably some lies."

"What about?"

"Things seen in the sky. I'm meeting a pilot here. He should be here in... actually he's already late."

The landlord stepped out from behind the bar. "Things seen in the sky, eh?"

"That's right."

"My uncle told me something he saw once."

"Really?" Roger looked up from the maps and collected images.

"It must have been just before the Great War. He'd come out of this very pub. And as he was walking home he heard a strange, low, trumpeting noise like one of them colliery bands tuning up. Strange thing was it was coming from above. So he stopped and looked up and saw this shadow above him. High up in the night sky, but blocking a great portion out, like a great bird. Then all of a sudden the sound stopped and it disappeared. The '*giant ghost bird*' he called it."

"When was this?"

"Not sure. Must've been about 1913. 'E was about 23 year old. Afore 'e lost 'is arm at Mametz."

Roger nodded. He opened up a spiral notebook, scribbled down a few words, a date and a location before ripping off the page and placing it on the outskirts of the map. The landlord peered at the vast display that covered the table.

"Lucky we han't got many in today," he mumbled amiably. "That's a lot of nonsense you have there."

Roger grinned. "Almost too much."

He pointed at a photograph with the date, "1964" and the location, "Above Fylingdales" next to it and started to explain the relevance of each image around the map.

1964 –Above Fylingdales

A plane of an unknown type is seen in the sky above Fylingdales. Crews are scrambled and anti-aircraft ordinance readied. The plane in question looks something like a Lancaster Bomber (obsolete by the late 1940s). There is a great deal of back and forth between the R.A.F. and Whitehall. The order is given to shoot it down. The report states that as the searchlight finds the plane and the anti-aircraft crew find their target, the plane disappears.

<u>1959 – *The Black Swan* - Pickering</u>

Bernard Jenkins tumbles out of *The Black Swan* at closing time to find two lights floating above him in the sky. He calls out to his companion and the landlady who also witness this phenomenon. There is a very loud roaring sound. They assume it is a plane, though the sound of the engines is much louder than normal. The lights and sound suddenly cease. If the sound had continued they would have assumed that the plane had gone behind a cloud. But the sudden ceasing of the noise makes the silence vast and jarring. The landlady invites Bernard and his companion back into the pub where they spend several hours and more pints trying to explain the experience.

285

<u>1912 – Whitby Bay</u>

At 12 noon on January 7th an enormous vibration shakes the windows of the houses in the town for thirty-five seconds. The old glass in the top windows of the Villa Rosa crack and have to be replaced at the cost of three shillings and sixpence. A vast shadow passes over the Abbey and out into the bay before flickering and vanishing along with the vibrations.

<u>1908 – The School House - Sleights</u>

Miss Stanton, the school-mistress, is finishing her mid-morning cup of tea when a loud bang causes her to rush to the playground. Once outside she finds all twenty-seven of her children lying on their fronts with their hands over their ears. On questioning the children she finds most of them tearful and incoherent, though several of them report a "swooping shadow." Most of the children report hearing difficulties for several weeks, though Miss Stanton notes that only tends to be when she asks them to tidy the play area.

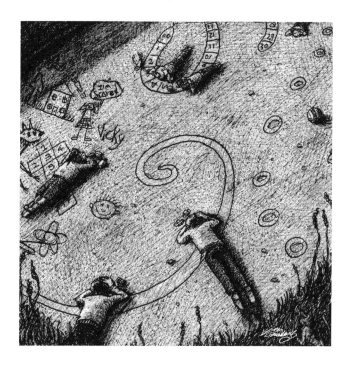

The churchwarden and his wife are snuffing out candles after Evensong, when a strange rumbling outside causes the final candles to flicker. The vicar, who is finishing off the final communion wine, lest heathens use it for their wicked rituals, also hears the commotion and the three of them venture outside. They see, what the vicar later describes as, *"a vast dark angel flying flat against the moon."* The windows of the church shudder. Some of the old mortar has to be repaired the following week at the cost of over four shillings. The vicar notes in his own diary that he considers the builder to be something of a scoundrel to charge so much.

1752 – Falling Foss Waterfall – Littlebeck

As Master John Letterton spies upon Mary Tasker bathing in the pool at the foot of the falls, his foot slips. His position in the bush is revealed somewhat as he tumbles upon his back and rips his breeches. Mary grabs her petticoat and covers herself quickly, cursing loudly at the peeping boy, when, what they later describe to the local priest, as "*the roar of a monster*", is heard. Far above their heads a vast winged shape flickers into being before disappearing again. Once their tale is fully recounted to the local priest, Mary, now recovered, remembers to give Master John a hearty slap.

1704 – Ruswarp

A coach pulls to a stop with a cry from the coachman and a loud whinnying complaint from the horses. The coachman, Mr Christopher Stanley and three passengers, who are identified as Jeremy Pargiter (an accountant from Pickering), Sir Stanley Berry (a minor composer) and Edward Rythe (occupation unknown) are surprised that the sounds of the coach coming to a stop are drowned out by a tremendous crashing roar above their heads. A vast shadow falls over the road, but looking up all they can see is a blurred black shape with the light of the sun bleeding around its edges.

<u>1656 – Sneaton Castle</u>

In his private diaries, found in the priest hole at Sneaton, an anonymous priest tells of a time that he was rushed and locked into his hiding place by his Papist host, where he remained for several hours before his release. In the diary entry he writes of becoming aware of voices and movement around the house, of a shouting and clattering of doors. After a while these sounds lessen and fade completely. In what he thinks is the third hour of his incarceration he describes the house as "*shaking terribly*" and the wood panel "*trembling*" in tandem with a "*deep and awful found that muft have emanated from hell itfelf.*"

On his release he questions his host on the matter and is told that both his host and the priest's potential persecutors had been *"fore affrighted by a terrible winged demon"* that *"appeared in the weft, flew acroff the fky for a few moments before vanishing behind a cloud and not reappearing."* They report that the sound suddenly stopped as it went behind the cloud. After this strange phenomenon the Protestant soldiers lost their taste for his capture and so, for the time being at least, the priest remains safe.

The landlord gestured with his head to the door at a young man in military uniform. Roger stood up. The pilot did not move from the door.

"Would you like to come and sit down?"

The pilot shook his head. Roger moved to the door. The pilot whispered to him.

"I am sorry. I cannot stay. I thought it impolite not to at least come and tell you."

"Tell me what?"

The pilot glanced through the window at the black car waiting outside. The doors of the car all opened together and three men wearing black bowler hats climbed out in unison, shutting the doors before standing in front of the car, staring at the inn.

"I did not know. I am not permitted to speak of what I saw."

"What did you see?"

"I must leave. It is not permitted for me to say more. I just thought you should know."

Roger nodded. "Don't worry yourself. I have had dealings with these Whitehall cronies before. Official secrets I suppose. Shame. I was just building a coherent picture of something."

The men outside started to walk towards the inn.

"I must leave," the pilot said again. "But one thing I will say. Those things you have told me about. The details of previous sightings. That is permitted. They will allow that, but anything further will reveal too much of what will be – even sharing my own experience."

Roger nodded again. "You know I will write that down."

The pilot smiled, "It is too cryptic to cause them worry."

The door started to push open. The pilot nodded his head slightly before opening the door fully. He pushed past the three bowler-hatted men roughly, walking past the car and up the road towards Whitby. The three bowler-hatted men doffed their hats at the landlord and Roger, then, as one, they turned on their heels and walked to the car. The pilot's form began to shrink into the distance. Roger and the landlord watched for some time as the car followed the pilot at a walking pace. As it pulled level with him, the window wound down. The pilot waved the car away and continued to walk. The car, however, kept pace, following the pilot until he hopped over a stile and wandered into a nearby field. The car sat idly for a moment. A door opened. One of the bowler-hatted men got out and opened the gate next to the stile. Once the car was driven onto the field and the gate shut behind it, Roger and the landlord turned from the window.

As Roger tidied away his maps and notes the landlord put a glass of ale in front of him.

"I hate to see a man look so downhearted."

"It's a shame," Roger sighed. "But it's not unexpected."

"I wonder what he knew," the landlord pondered, picking up an empty glass from a nearby table.

"Almost too much," whispered Roger.

A roar of engines shook the windows as the shadow of a plane drifted over the landscape, skimming the sloping hills in the distance and turning the pinks of the heather to dark purple in its shade. Roger glanced up briefly to note its passing.

"It must be twelve thirty," the landlord muttered. Roger continued to tidy his notes away.

The pilot in question was never identified, though a story did surface in the mid-1980s concerning a pilot who witnessed the appearance of a strange and unfamiliar plane whilst on a training flight over the North York Moors. Apparently the pilot was part of a test of the early warning system. He spoke of a plane suddenly appearing out of a bank of high cloud. The plane then seemed to blink in and out of his vision, disappearing and reappearing in flickers over a few seconds until, when it was only several hundred feet away, it disappeared for good.

About the Author

Chris Lambert – Storyteller – Teacher – Traveller of Mist – Mythogeographer – Demiurge - Liar

Chris Lambert is the curator of the Black Meadow and its associated phenomena. He works closely with Kev Oyston as part of "The Soulless Party" to uncover the mysteries hidden within its dense mist.

He writes far too much. As well as the critically lauded Tales from the Black Meadow, Wyrd Kalendar and Songs from the Black Meadow he has also had short stories published in The Ghastling, The Dead Files and Tales of the Damned. He has had four plays published and over 20 performed professionally including: The Simple Process of Alchemy, Loving Chopin and Ship of Fools. He occasionally dabbles with music too.

For more of Lambert visit:
Blackmeadowtales.blogspot.co.uk
Musicforzombies.blogspot.co.uk
Lambertthewriter.blogspot.co.uk

About the Illustrators

Andy Paciorek is a graphic artist and writer, drawn mainly to the worlds of myth, folklore, symbolism, decadence, curiosa, anomaly, dark romanticism and otherworldly experience. He is fascinated both by the beautiful and the grotesque and the twilight threshold consciousness where these boundaries blur. The mist-gates, edges and liminal zones where nature borders supernature and daydreams and nightmares cross paths are of great inspiration.

He has worked for various clients and outlets including Harper Collins, Cumbrian Cthulhu and Wyrd Harvest Press.

He is also the creator of the Folk Horror Revival project.

Nigel Wilson is an artist, singer, actor and prop-maker.

He illustrated "Tales from the Black Meadow", "Christmas on the Black Meadow" and "Some Words with a Mummy". He plays a fantastic Father Christmas and has a beautiful bass singing voice.

John Chadwick is a writer, illustrator, animation filmmaker, spoken word performer and former co-host of Drawing Out the Spirits podcast. A former university senior lecturer and writer/illustrator in residence at The Yorkshire Sculpture Park, his work has been exhibited, published and performed through several medium since his film Spiritual Love was nominated for Young Narrative Filmmaker of the Year at the 1996 British Short Film Festival. His influences have always been spirituality, the paranormal and forteana. This has led him into investigation, research and practice in several related fields. As an experiencer he also believes in healthy scepticism. He is a Dischordian Pope as well as a Minister for the Church of the Subgenius.

The Black Meadow Archive

After years of campaigning the Brightwater Archive has finally been opened. From the recesses of these hidden filing cabinets and dusty boxes the sounds of the Black Meadow pour like the ever pervading mist that hangs over the moors.

Created alongside the book of the same name this new album steps into new hauntological vistas exploring White Horses, Coyles and Ghosts of the distant past, sweeping through the bramble and heather before bringing into sharp focus the more recent tragedies that have beset those who dare to wander from the path into the Black Meadow.

Available from Castles in Space.

When Professor R. Mullins of the University of York went missing in 1972 on the site of the area known as Black Meadow atop of the North Yorkshire Moors, he left behind him an extensive body of work that provided a great insight into the folklore of this mysterious place.

Writer Chris Lambert has been rooting through Mullins' files for over ten years and now presents this collection of weird and macabre tales.

Marvel at tales such as The Rag and Bone Man, The Meadow Hag, The Fog House, The Land Spheres and The Children of the Black Meadow.

What is the mystery surrounding The Coalman and the Creature?

Who or what is The Watcher in the Village?

What is the significance of the Shining Apples?

Why is it dangerous to watch the Horsemen dance?

Beautifully illustrated by Nigel Wilson these tales will haunt you for a long time to come.

"The stand out entries include "Beyond the Moor" a poem about a maiden accosted by a bandit who remains unafraid due to having been to the "beyond" of the title and returned. Also of note are "Children of the Black Meadow" where a bereaved mother resurrects her deceased kids as blackberry bramble homunculi; cyclical damnation tale "The Coal Man and the Creature" and the paranoia-inducing sucker punch "The Watcher From the Village" ... this is a collection that strongly invites a second reading.." - STARBURST MAGAZINE

"...visceral dread slowly rises from its mustiness..." – *Mythogeography*

"A fine piece of British Hauntology" - Gareth Rees Author of Marshland

"Properly spooky and really well written." - Sebastian Baczkiewicz - Creator of Radio 4's Pilgrim

Exiled Publications – Available from Amazon

Professor R. Mullins, a classics professor, had a great interest in Black Meadow, in particular its folklore and spent many years documenting its history and tales that were part of the local oral tradition. In his office, his colleagues found over twenty thick notebooks crammed with stories and interviews from the villages around Black Meadow.

Some of these stories seemed to be from the legendary disappearing village itself and provided some vital clues as to how the phenomena was interpreted and explained by the local populace.

In 1978, Radio 4 produced a now rare documentary about the folklore, mystery and tales surrounding the Black Meadow area. It also featured music specially commissioned to accompany the programme. This music has recently been unearthed by the Mullins Estate and carefully isolated for your listening pleasure.

These stories, poems and songs have also been gathered together to capture the unsettling nature of the Black Meadow.

Do not listen to this on your own at night and make sure you shut your windows. Listen for the stamping feet of the horsemen, avoid the gaze of the Watcher in the village and do not walk into the mist.

"... it could have been copied from a vinyl record from the '70s.... atmospheric precision..."
Starburst Magazine

"It's a gratifyingly atmospheric listen, filled with processed choral eeriness and murky radiophonic unease- a psychogeographic essential." – Electronic Sound

Available to download from Bandcamp

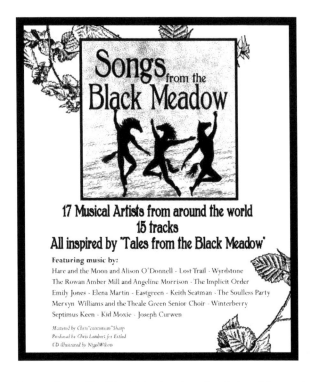

17 Musical Artists from around the world
15 tracks
All inspired by "Tales from the Black Meadow"

Featuring music by:

Hare and the Moon and Alison O'Donnell - Lost Trail - Wyrdstone
The Rowan Amber Mill and Angeline Morrison - The Implicit Order
Emily Jones - Elena Martin - Eastgreen - Keith Seatman - The Soulless Party
Mervyn Williams - The Theale Green Senior Choir - Winterberry
Septimus Keen - Kid Moxie - Joseph Curwen

Mastered by Chris "cancerman" Sharp
Produced by Chris Lambert for Exiled
CD illustrated by Nigel Wilson

"Songs From The Black Meadow is a deeply involving and atmospherically congruent undertaking, swathed in the beckoning hauntology of the fictitious-or-is-it Black Meadow itself." - **Record Collector**

"Sometimes frivolous, sometimes chilling, let this be your entrance into one of modern acid folk's most pervasive myths." – **Goldmine Magazine**

Released by Mega Dodo
All profits go to Cancer Research UK
www.mega-dodo.co.uk

A book is also available from Amazon

It is Christmas on the North York Moors. The snow sits upon the heather and bramble. The fences around RAF Fylingdales are silent and still. A dense mist grows in the distance. If you listen closely you can hear strange Yuletide chants, the hum of a land sphere and the cackle of a meadow hag.

This collection of Christmas tales from the Black Meadow contains three new Yuletide stories.

Experience a beautiful inversion of The Nativity in A Black Meadow Christmas, warm your toes in a tale of matriarchal terror in The Meadow Tree and marvel at the delightful wonders of The Black Star. You will also find details of ideal gifts you could give and games that you can play when visiting the Black Meadow.

With beautiful illustrations by Andy Paciorek and Nigel Wilson, this is a festive treat that will bring joy and fear in equal measure to your Christmas celebrations.

All profits from the sale of this book go to Worldwide Cancer Research.

Published by Exiled – Available from Amazon and all good bookshops.

Lambert · Paciorek

Wyrd Kalendar

Hold to the resolution in January...
Seek to do more with those missing days in February...
Avoid the madness of the March hare...
Become the fool in April...
Dance around Aunt May...
Protect and nurture the June bug...
Celebrate Grotto Day in July...
Fall in love and weep in August...
Let it all fall in September...
Prepare for the October harvest...
Avoid November sin...
Do not let December find you out...

Open the Wyrd Kalendar and explore the year with eyes that are not your own...

Join Chris Lambert and Andy Paciorek as they guide you through the twelve months of the year weaving twelve tales of Magic, Murder, Terror, Love and the Wyrd.

"Gripping, sometimes terrifying but always surprising: this is the year described in the Wyrd Kalendar. Live it if you dare..." –
Sebastian Baczkiewicz - Creator of BBC Radio 4's "Pilgrim"

"If you like your scare fare laced with imagination, surprise, and plenty of spine-tingling moments, I cannot recommend this enough"- Scream Magazine

"...this package represents a thriving literary and musical counter-culture." **** SHINDIG

Published by Wyrd Harvest Press
Album available to download from Mega Dodo

BLACK EARTH
A FIELD GUIDE TO
THE SLAVIC OTHERWORLD

BY
ANDREW L. PACIOREK

Following on in the footsteps of Strange Lands: A Field Guide to the Celtic Otherworld, Black Earth guides the curious on a fully illustrated journey into the strange Otherworld of the Slavic nations.

Wondered whose eyes are glaring at you in the bathhouse or who is lurking in the deep dark birch woods and the golden grain fields? What lies beneath the damp black earth? Wonder no more, let Andrew L. Paciorek guide you into the worlds beyond.

Safe return not guaranteed...

Available from Blurb

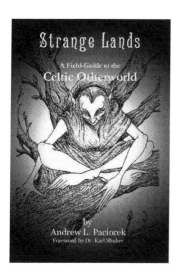

Strange Lands

A Field-Guide to the
Celtic Otherworld

by
Andrew L. Paciorek
Foreword by Dr. Karl Shuker

Strange Lands by Andrew Paciorek is a deeply researched and richly illustrated information guide to the entities and beasts of Celtic myth & legend and to the many strange beings that have entered the lore of the land through the influence of other cultures and technological evolution.

At nearly 400 pages and featuring over 170 original illustrations, Strange Lands is an essential accompaniment for both the novice and seasoned walkers between worlds.

Available from Blurb

The Human Chimaera
Andrew Paciorek
Containing over 100 original pen & ink portraits alongside biographic text, The Human Chimaera is an indispensable guide to the greatest stars of the circus sideshows and dime museums.
Includes a foreword by John Robinson of Sideshow World.

Available from Blurb

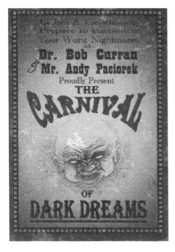

The Carnival of Dark Dreams
Dr Bob Curran & Andy Paciorek

Welcome to The Carnival of Dark Dreams. A visual daytrip into the depths of the jungle, the sands of the desert, to many haunted habitats and worse still into the darkness of the human imagination. But fear not, for captured, caged and presented for your curiosity by Dr. Bob Curran and Mr. Andy Paciorek are some of the most deadly, grotesque, fearsome entities of world folklore. Dare you visit The Carnival of Dark Dreams?

Wyrd Harvest Press

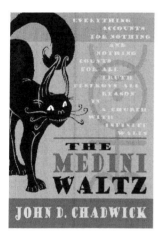

The Medini Waltz
John Chadwick

The Medini Waltz is possibly the first Zen, gothic, metaphysical, psychedelic, quantum, supernatural, comedy ever written. Chadwick has created a mind-bending journey full of art heists, magic, gods & goddesses, demons & parallel worlds, with the edge of Robert Anton Wilson, the comedy of Douglas Adams, the character of Mervyn Peake, the horror of Dennis Wheatley, the wisdom of Paulo Coelho and a distinct voice all of his own.

Available from Lulu

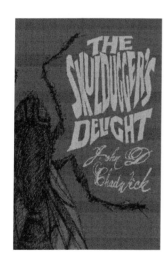

The Skulldugger's Delight
John Chadwick

Follow the twisting trail of countless murders in this 18th century mystery embroiled with conspiracy, embezzlement, cannibalism and supernatural revenge. Enter the grotesque world of master storyteller John D. Chadwick in this deliciously blood soaked, black comedy in the tradition of the penny dreadful.

Available from Lulu

307

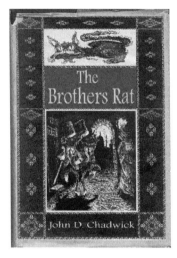

The Brothers Rat
John Chadwick

Join Jim Slaney & Patrick Murphy on their drunken revelry, as they carouse the phantasmagorias, grope ladies of the night and plunge into the hellish depths of London, on a quest for the ultimate opiate. Withnail and I meets Jack the Ripper by way of H.P Lovecraft in this comic, steampunk, psychedelic trip, rife with Victorian horror, freaks and devilish intent.

Available from Lulu

The Theosophical Teapot
John Chadwick

Disturbing, comic and gruesome tales drawing on fringe personalities from the darkest corners of humanity. Meet the Society of Jack The Ripper's, people embroiled in Black Magic, revolutionary protesters, compulsive obsessives and a man determined to assassinate the reincarnation of Adolf Hitler aided by the voices in his head. John D. Chadwick is one of those writers who could change the way you see the world forever.

Available from Lulu

308

Printed in Great Britain
by Amazon